# To A Blissful Christmas Reunion

# Timeslip Romance

# Lucy knelt beside Gabe's prostrate body.

She leant close. Yes, he was still breathing. He didn't look great. But he didn't look worse, either.

She folded the duvet double and tucked it round him. Then she put her raincoat over the top. It didn't matter if Lucy got cold. Or wet. What mattered was to compensate for the wet and cold coming up from the ground he was lying on.

She wanted to take him in her arms and hug him. But he mustn't be moved. At the same time, she wanted to thump him for his stupidity. She couldn't do that, either, so she raged at him, instead. "What on earth were you playing at, Gabe? You know cedars are dangerous in a storm. But you were only thinking about saving your precious tree, weren't you?" She swallowed tears of an emotion she didn't want to identify. "Oh, Gabe, you— One day, someone is going to tell you you're a prize idiot. Lovable, yes, but an idiot."

She fancied his lashes flickered a tiny bit just then. Oh help, had he heard what she'd just said? Please, no. She couldn't possibly face him if he knew how she felt about him. It would be humiliating.

Not daring to breathe, she fixed her eyes on his face.

His eyes didn't open. There was no sign at all that he was coming round.

Lucy knew she shouldn't be relieved, but she was.

*To Margaret*
*with love.*
*Joanna M*
*aka Evelyn*
*xx.*

# TO A BLISSFUL
# CHRISTMAS
# REUNION

## ~Timeslip Romance~

## JOANNA MAITLAND

Published in the United Kingdom
by Joanna Maitland Independent
https://libertabooks.com

To a Blissful Christmas Reunion
Timeslip Romance
Revised & Extended Second Edition
Previously published by Libertà Books as: *One Christmas Tree to Go*

Requests to publish work from this book should be made to:
info@LibertaBooks.com

Cover Design: Joanna Maitland
Cover Images stock.adobe.com:
marchello74; olenachukhil; neirfy
Interior Formatting: Joanna Maitland

# Chapter One

GABE FIRMED THE SOIL around the last sapling with his boot. He straightened gratefully, stretching his arms to ease his aching back.

On impulse, he knelt back down by the little silver conifer and patted it lovingly. "Grow, little tree," he said. "You and your mates can make this nursery thrive." In his mind, he added, "*Please* grow," but he didn't say that aloud. It was bad enough that he was talking to his trees; if someone heard him pleading with them, they'd think he was fit for the funny farm rather than his own tree farm.

"Gabe?"

He jerked to his feet so fast he almost overbalanced. Lucy. Of course, it would have to be Lucy. The very last person he wanted to catch him talking to his plants.

He managed a rueful smile in response to her puzzled expression. "Miss Cairns. Nice to see you. What can I do for you?"

She made a face. "You can stop being so formal, for

starters, Gabriel Bliss, as I've said before. I call you 'Gabe'. What's so wrong with you calling me 'Lucy'?"

"Everything, as you know perfectly well," Gabe said flatly. "I'm your father's tenant here. So you're pretty much my employer."

"Gabe, that's rubbish and—"

"No, it's not. It's part of the respect I owe your father. And since you're his number two in the business, I'd say 'Miss Cairns' was appropriate, wouldn't you?" Why did she keep refusing to understand? She knew the risk her father had taken by giving Gabe the lease on such a huge chunk of his land. Not many successful businessmen would do that for someone with no track record as an entrepreneur. Not many successful businessmen would charge peanuts in rent and give the lessee a totally free hand, either. Gabe hoped that, by the time Lucy took over the estate, the nursery would be profitable enough to pay a decent rent—if it wasn't, Gabe would probably be bankrupt—but his gut was telling him that it was vital to keep a *professional* relationship with her, at least as long as his business was still struggling.

She snorted. "That stubborn pride will be the death of you one of these days, Gabe. Dad's in his prime and you know it. So I'll probably be old and grey before I inherit, and a good thing too. Right now, there's no reason why we can't be friends." She smiled encouragingly. She was stunning when she smiled. Gabe realised in that moment that her intricately-tied silk scarf exactly matched the blue of her eyes. They were smiling, too.

Gabe managed a shrug and automatically took a step back. He needed that extra distance. Lucy Cairns might imagine they could have a no-strings friendship but Gabe knew better. She wasn't only his boss's daughter; she was also much too attractive for any man's equilibrium.

2

Especially one who was, in old-fashioned terms, just a menial. Dirty-fingered tree-planters did not consort with the daughters of their millionaire landlords.

"Friendship is for equals," he managed at last, through a dry throat. "You and I are..." He gestured helplessly with open hands. "Best if we keep things businesslike. So, what can I do for you?"

Lucy responded with a noise that tried to be an angry growl. Gabe thought she sounded like a cuddly puppy, doing a wolf impression. He said nothing, waiting.

Finally, she sighed and said, matter-of-factly, "Christmas trees. Or, more specifically, *one* Christmas tree. A really special one this year. I want to put a tree into the stairwell so that our guests can admire it all the way up to the top floor."

"Four floors worth of tree?"

She nodded, grinning. "Yes, and broad enough to be touched by reaching over the banisters. Don't you think it'll look great? And that gorgeous smell will fill the house."

"Um. Yes, I suppose so. But we're talking forty feet, maybe more. That's a helluva tree. How do you plan to get it in? Assuming I can find one big enough, of course."

"Oh, we'll manage. Dad'll send some of the builders over to help, if I ask him."

"Ah. So you haven't actually cleared this idea with your father?"

Lucy waved a hand airily. "He leaves all the house arrangements to me. The Boxing Day Shoot is my part of the business so he won't interfere. And he'll *adore* it once he sees how fabulous it looks. And smells."

Her father wouldn't adore it half so much if his precious antiques were damaged while the monster tree

3

was being dragged into place, but it would do no good to say so to Lucy. She was always full of off-the-wall schemes and her father indulged them. Usually. A lot of them, Gabe had to admit, had been very successful. Besides, Gabe could make a pretty decent profit on selling her a forty-foot Christmas tree. It would help to finance the purchase of the rare young trees he'd had his eye on to enlarge the specialist collection in his nursery.

"OK. You're the client. I'll look around and see what I can find. But you need to give me a better idea of the finished height before I earmark one of the biggest trees in the old plantation for the axe. There aren't many backup buyers for a forty-footer if you suddenly decide it's too short. Trafalgar Square won't be buying a spare tree from me, you know." He grinned at his own joke, though he knew it wasn't very funny.

She narrowed her eyes at him. She wasn't laughing. "The Trafalgar Square tree is a lot bigger than forty feet. What's more, we both know it comes from Norway. And why."

"Yes, sorry. Bad joke. Forget I said it. Still, if you give me a finished height, I'll have something to work with. We can always lop a bit off the bottom if the tree's too tall. Can you drop a tape from the top of the stairwell?"

'You don't give me much credit, do you, Gabe? You forget that I've been running the house and the antiques side of the business for more than five years now. I do know about practicalities. The height from the hall floor to the ceiling at the top of the stairwell is forty-four feet ten inches."

"Oh. Um. Yes, right." He couldn't meet her eyes. He was sure she'd be laughing at him now.

"And, before you ask, the maximum diameter of the

bottom of the tree is sixteen feet four inches. Though I suppose we could always trim the lower branches if the tree was too bushy at the bottom."

"That might look ugly, if it isn't carefully done." Gabe saw that Lucy had raised an eloquent eyebrow. "But I'm sure you'll do a great job. Or I could do it for you?" he added, in a rush to make amends. He really ought to know better than to imply that Lucy Cairns was incompetent. Because it wasn't true. She seemed to succeed at everything she did, blast her. It was another one of the reasons why he could never be totally easy in her company, these days. Why did Sir Andrew Cairns's only child have to be such a fanciable female? If Lucy had been a Luke, Gabe might have been able to get over their differences in status and wealth. Gabe and a male Cairns heir might have been friends. But Lucy was too attractive by half. No red-blooded male was going to look at her and think "friend". No way.

Lucy smiled at him then. "That's kind of you, Gabe. Let's decide once you've found a suitable tree. And now comes the tricky part. How much?"

Gabe did a quick calculation, added a large but not outrageous mark-up to his normal price per foot of tree, and named his figure. Lucy didn't look shocked. She just nodded. Double blast. He'd missed a trick there. He could have got more towards his rare specimen trees. He couldn't jack the price up now—that would be highly unprofessional—but there was one last wrinkle he could use. "And—sorry—but I'll have to charge you for the full height of the tree we fell, not just the cut-down height. We might have to fell a sixty-footer to get one to fit your stairwell."

"Of course," Lucy said graciously. "Let me have the bill and I'll make sure it's paid promptly. And—this isn't a reflection on you, Gabe, honestly—but I'd like to come and see the tree before it's cut. I've got a bit of a thing about Christmas trees, you see, and this one's going to be very special. I want to… I'd like to see it while it's still growing. So I can—" She made a wry face and shrugged helplessly.

"You want to talk to it while it can still hear you?" he asked softly. It was what he himself did, every time he felled a tree. Killing a living thing, even in a good cause, required an apology, or at least an explanation. It didn't really surprise him that she felt the same way. They had always been on the same wavelength. Before.

"Sounds sentimental, doesn't it?" Lucy said ruefully. "Can't help it, I'm afraid. I'll probably stroke it as well. And here's me, making myself out to be the hard businesswoman. You've rumbled me, Gabriel Bliss. Just don't shop me to any of my other suppliers, hmm? I know you understand, but I'd never hear the end of it from the others." There was a bit of colour on her neck above that azure blue scarf. The blush made her look much younger, like an endearing child caught out in mischief.

Gabe only just managed to stop himself from reaching out to stroke her arm. "Your secret's safe with me," he said gruffly. "I'll give you a ring once I've selected your tree. But we shouldn't fell it until just before Christmas, if we want it to be looking really good on Boxing Day. OK by you?"

"Fine. We've got a deal." She pulled off her leather glove and stuck out her hand.

Automatically, Gabe responded. Her fingers were warm against his and her skin was very soft. She didn't seem to mind the ingrained dirt on his fingers or the calluses on his palm.

The contact was brief and very businesslike. A few seconds later, she had climbed back into her battered old Land Rover and was driving away with a cheery wave.

"Lucy Cairns," Gabe muttered grimly to the sapling nestled against his mud-covered boot, "is good enough to eat. Unfortunately, she's much too rich a diet for the likes of me." He sighed and went to collect another bale of conifer saplings. The light would be going soon and he'd nowhere near finished his day's work.

Lucy was grinding her teeth even before she was back on the tarmac lane and out of sight. Honestly, the man was impossible. Totally impossible. Her father would have used much more down-to-earth words, if he'd heard that exchange. Drew Cairns was a shrewd northern businessman and he believed in calling a spade a spade. Or, in his words, "a bloody shovel". Lucy was tempted to call Gabriel Bliss a self-righteous prig, except that no one used that kind of language, nowadays. It was a very satisfying insult, but it belonged to a different time.

"They did a good line in abuse, back then," she said aloud. The Land Rover didn't answer. "Pity no one would appreciate it, these days."

She wasn't sure that was true. Gabe was wedded to the land and to growing his beloved trees, but he was very well read. Although Lucy loved English literature and read the classics avidly, she'd been caught out more than once by Gabe's exceptional memory. He'd corrected her about George Eliot's *Middlemarch*, she recalled, though it was years ago now. She'd argued back, but when she checked, she'd discovered he was right. She'd swallowed her pride and gone back to apologise.

She smiled to herself, reliving that old encounter for a moment. She'd been wrong but Gabe hadn't tried to rub it in. He hadn't been superior at all, though he probably had a right to be. He simply put an arm round her shoulder and gave her a quick hug. Then he grinned at her and said that he'd just been lucky that that particular bit of Eliot had stuck in his mind, and that Lucy was usually right when they argued about books. She remembered the warm glow, the feeling of being valued. But that was back when they were friends. Back when they were equals, in spite of her father's increasing wealth. Back in the days before Gabe took on the nursery lease and Sir Andrew Cairns and his daughter became "the bosses".

"Men!" she spat. "Why do they have to have so much stiff-necked pride?"

The Land Rover backfired. Lucy jumped.

Then she laughed, a little shakily. "Thank you, Maisie. It's nice to know you agree with me. If you have any ideas about how I can make Gabe see sense about our friendship, I'd really like to hear them." She waited a second or two, but Maisie was back to chugging along in her usual rhythm. "No, I thought not," Lucy sighed. "For this particular idiot man, I'll have to find my own solutions."


"You look whacked, Gabe," Jane said as soon as he appeared in the nursery's checkout-cum-farmshop.

Gabe automatically bent down to fondle Muffin's silky ears. Strictly speaking, the black and tan mongrel was Jane's dog, but he treated Gabe's nursery as if he owned it. He only had three legs, but he never let that stop him being a feisty little fellow. Gabe was very fond of Muffin, because he was a fighter, in the best possible sense.

Jane automatically started for the tiny kitchen at the back. "I'll make us a cup of tea if you mind the till for me. Probably won't be any more customers today, anyway. Too cold for them to venture out, poor darlings," she added, with more than a hint of sarcasm. Jane might be motherly to Gabe, but she came from solid farming stock and she didn't have much time for Lucy's pampered clients. "People with more money than sense," Jane called them.

Gabe was too tired to argue. Besides, Jane would ignore him even if he did. And she was right about the customers, pretty much. They included the many rich folk who visited the big house to browse and buy from Sir Andrew's vast antique collection. When they were leaving, Lucy always made a point of suggesting that they call in at the nursery where they would be sure to find excellent quality trees, some of them quite rare. Gabe had to admit that Lucy was a first-class saleswoman. With her moneyed clients, she would hint, ever so subtly, that Gabe's nursery could sell them something that none of their friends could possibly have. And Gabe had secured some quite lucrative sales as a result. He owed her for those.

But she was still his landlord's daughter.

"Here you go." Jane re-emerged with two steaming mugs and put them on the wooden counter by the till. "And I think we'll have a couple of biscuits to go with it." She gave Gabe a sly smile. "Those farmhouse gingers haven't sold too well. I reckon the last two packs are nearly on their sell-by date."

Gabe laughed and sank on to one of the wicker stools behind the checkout. "I'll never make any money if we keep eating the stock, you know." They both knew he was joking. Jane had definitely made a mistake with the farmhouse gingers: too expensive for their everyday customers and not at all the kind of thing that Lucy's antique buyers would bother with. No doubt they had cooks and housekeepers to do mundane chores like shopping for biscuits. They probably had garden staff as well. So what did the gardeners think when the boss chose a vastly expensive specimen tree without consulting them?

Actually, Gabe knew the answer to that one. He'd been one of those hired gardeners himself, until not so long ago. He'd toiled for three years making his first employer's estate look fantastic, but the man never so much as passed the time of day with any of the staff. That applied especially to people like Gabe, who wasn't even the head man, just a dirty-fingered assistant minion. When the owner showed his garden off to his guests, he implied that all the design and planting innovations were his own. And his wife was even worse. She would walk round the garden in spindly high heels, complaining that they sank into the meandering grass paths. Finally, she persuaded her more-money-than-sense husband to have the sinuous paths ripped up and replaced with solid paving slabs. It didn't bother her, or her husband, that the contractors did a vast amount of damage to the plants while they were driving around with their diggers. Or that the dreamy, drifty look of the garden was ruined by what seemed to be acres of grey concrete. Gabe was thoroughly disheartened to see the damage. And more than glad to leave when he was offered the job of head gardener on another estate. He planned to make his mark there. And to create something lasting and beautiful.

His hopes were soon dashed. His employer turned out to be another jumped-up, get-rich-quick merchant who enjoyed lording it over his staff. Gabe did his best to avoid the man and put his heart and soul into making the garden into something close to his vision of what was possible. It took a few years but it was finally beginning to bear fruit when, one day, the owner turned up, pleased as punch with the incredibly rare rhododendron he'd just acquired, at vast cost. Gabe had shaken his head and said that it would soon die in the estate's non-acid soil. He'd added, truthfully but naively, that his boss's purchase was a waste of money and the shrub should be sent back.

Not a good move. Gabe's second employer wasn't the kind of man who would ever admit to having made a mistake. Especially to a menial. He didn't lose his rag, though, or even raise his voice. He simply fired Gabe, on the spot, with clinical efficiency.

So the answer for those poor put-upon gardeners was to smile and tell the boss how clever he was. And then to work desperately to create growing conditions for the new tree in a spot where it wouldn't die. Or, at least, not until the boss had forgotten about its existence.

*How cynical I am*, Gabe thought, biting into one of the ginger biscuits. Muffin was gazing adoringly up at him. "Cupboard love," Gabe chuckled, giving the dog a piece when he thought Jane wasn't looking.

She was. She clucked her tongue and shook her head, but then she smiled and simply drank her tea.

Gabe told himself he wasn't being fair. Rich people weren't all ghastly, just because they were rich. They weren't all like his previous employers, either. Lucy and Drew Cairns were rolling in it, after all, and they were both fantastic. But then, Sir Andrew was a self-made man and a good judge of people. He wasn't swayed by wealth, either. And he'd brought Lucy up to think the same way.

"Was that Lucy's Land Rover earlier?" Jane asked. No "Miss Cairns" for her. She had known Lucy for nearly fifteen years and had mothered her for most of

11

them, after taking pity on the newly-widowed father and his only child. Drew Cairns had planned his family's move to the country as a reward for his wife—she had put up with years of hardship while her husband worked seven days a week to build up his construction business from nothing. Success had brought Drew financial security and, eventually, a knighthood, but Lucy's mother hadn't lived long enough to enjoy any of it. She'd died before she even had a chance to hear herself called "Lady Cairns".

And her daughter had been left motherless while she was still in primary school.

Gabe reckoned it was no wonder that Lucy and her father were close. Who else did Lucy have? Apart from Jane, of course. And, at a push—

"Gabe?" Jane prodded him in the chest with her half-empty tea mug. "You were miles away. About Lucy. Was that—?"

Motherly she might be, but Jane was also a terror for ferreting out gossip. She never gave up until her jaws were clamped round her prey. "Sorry," Gabe said quickly. "I was thinking about, er, the new trees. Yes, it was Lucy. She's got a new wheeze for Christmas. She wants a single enormous tree, one that's big enough to fill the whole stairwell."

Jane's eyes widened and she blew out a long, slow breath. "*All* of it?"

"Yup. All four floors."

Jane digested that for a minute or so and then said, "I hope you're charging her a premium price then, lovey. The Cairns estate can afford it and we need to make a profit on something."

"Oh, come on, Jane. You know we always make good money on the Christmas trees. And this year should be even better than usual, because we've got all those fabulous little trees in pots. The kids will adore them and their parents will buy them because it makes them feel virtuous to buy a cute little Christmas tree that won't end up on the bonfire. Placating the kids *and* doing their bit for the planet, you know?"

Jane shook her head. "Not doing their bit for your nursery, Gabe. Sure, we'll make good money out of it this year, but what about next year? What about when your virtuous parents all fetch their cute little potted trees in from the garden and decorate them again? When none of them come here to get a Bliss Christmas tree because they've *already got one*?"

She had a point, sort of, but Gabe wasn't about to concede. He knew his customers too well. "Most of them haven't a clue how to look after a conifer in a small pot. Quite a lot of the trees will die. Or else they'll drop so many of their needles that they'll not be fit to decorate. I guarantee you, Jane—" he dropped his biscuit hand to his side and tried to cross his fingers "—that more than half of those customers will be back for another tree next year."

"Humph." She didn't sound convinced. "How many potted trees do we have?"

"Not sure yet how many of them will be attractive enough to sell. A few dozen, maybe?"

Jane's shoulders relaxed. "That's something, at least. If it had been a hundred or more, you'd have had me really worried. Can't do too much harm with a couple of dozen. We'll still be selling loads of *proper* Christmas trees. The kind that go on the fire after Twelfth Night," she finished, with emphasis.

Gabe grinned at her. "Point taken," he said. "With you looking after my profits, Jane, I should be a millionaire by now. You're a first-class businesswoman, you know. And I'm really grateful for everything you do. I couldn't manage without you."

Jane coloured, a very little. "I'm not half as good a businesswoman as Lucy, though," she said. "Lucy would have known not to order these poncey ginger biscuits, but I didn't." She squared her shoulders. "Still, I do now and I'll be a lot more careful about the orders in the future. But what I do here in the shop is peanuts. We make far more profit from the clients that Lucy refers to us than from anything I do." Gabe opened his mouth to protest, but Jane wasn't going to let him get a word in edgeways. "You know I'm right, so don't try telling me otherwise, Gabriel Bliss. Lucy Cairns is a godsend for this place and we *owe* her. *You* owe her."

Jane was absolutely right, of course, but it didn't make the truth any more comfortable.

# Chapter Two

LUCY DROVE ROUND THE back of the Manor House and left the Land Rover in the yard with the keys in the ignition. All the staff were welcome to use it for getting around the estate or fetching and carrying, though some of them refused to try. Maisie was well known for her idiosyncrasies and Lucy was probably the only one who had any kind of a soft spot for the battered old four-by-four. Yes, the estate could certainly afford to replace Maisie but no, Lucy wasn't going to allow that. Not while there was still life left in dear old Maisie.

Lucy wasn't going to allow herself to dwell on the Gabriel Bliss problem, either. She had far more important things to do. She hadn't yet finalised all the details for the next pheasant shoot in less than a week's time. Around a dozen guns would be staying in the house for several days which would give Lucy plenty of opportunities to interest them (or their wives) in the antiques. Practically everything in the house was for sale, if the price was right, since she and her father had agreed, long ago, that none of their antiques had any sentimental value. If a guest wanted to buy the four-poster he was sleeping in, or the dining table where he ate, Lucy would happily negotiate a price. If the sold item was an essential for the running of the house, like a bed or a table, she would source a replacement antique from one of her contacts in the trade. And in due course, that replacement would probably be sold, too.

As a result of their odd way of living, the contents of the house never stayed the same for very long. But Lucy preferred it that way. The house was a showcase for the business, not a real home. Her only real home had been the cramped house where she grew up, the house they'd left that Christmas after her mother died. All their furniture and fittings, everything bar Lucy's toys and books, had been sold; Drew Cairns, deep in his grief, was adamant that he didn't want anything to remind him of what he had lost.

The only item not for sale now was the painting of her mother, hanging above the fireplace in the ground floor office. It lacked the vital spark of the best portraits—the artist had had to use photographs since Lucy's mother was long dead by the time Sir Andrew commissioned the work—but it was a good enough likeness and a reminder of a loving, and much loved, wife and mother. Lucy had occasionally walked into the office to find her father standing gazing at it. Once, she'd fancied there was a tear in his eye.

Today the office was empty since Pat, Lucy's PA, worked only three days a week. Lucy was glad to be alone. She had loads to do and she wasn't in the mood for idle chatter. Pat was very efficient and reliable—the business wouldn't be able to function properly without her— but she did like to talk while she was working.

Subtle hints about the value of silence were always a waste of breath.

Lucy sat down at her desk by the window and smiled up at her mother's portrait. Looking at it gave her a warm glow, almost like being hugged—she could still remember her mother's hugs and how special they had made her feel. She missed them, even now, after so many years.

Lucy pulled out the guest list for the pheasant shoot and ran her finger down it, counting the number of question marks against names. Several of the wives had been havering about whether to attend or not. They didn't shoot and they thought they would be bored while their husbands were out slaughtering birds. The house was much too far from any decent shopping unless they hired a helicopter—which their husbands wouldn't agree to, since the noise might disturb the shoot.

Lucy smiled grimly. She'd recently bought some very fine antique silk rugs but the colours and motifs were too feminine to appeal to the guns. Lucy needed the wives to attend—and to persuade their husbands to buy. Selecting a name from the list, the woman who was closest to being a fashion leader among the guests, Lucy picked up the phone and dialled.

"Mrs Fairbrother, good morning. It's Lucy Cairns here," she began. "I wanted to run a couple of ideas past you, about next week's shoot, if you have a moment. It's about the ladies' programme you suggested. I didn't want to finalise anything without asking your advice. Is now a good time?"

Mrs Fairbrother was sufficiently flattered to let Lucy run through the programme that had taken her two solid days to devise. The woman made a few suggestions, some helpful, some useless, but Lucy agreed them all. It needed to become so completely Mrs Fairbrother's programme that she would persuade all her fellow-ditherers to attend.

"Thank you so much, Mrs Fairbrother. That really rounds out your programme in ways I hadn't thought about. You're clearly an expert when it comes to organising events. I'd never have thought of a picnic at this time of year." Mrs Fairbrother made approving noises. "As you rightly said, though," Lucy went on, "a picnic in the old arboretum will depend on the weather. The forecast is good, but you never know. We'll have rugs and heaters, of course, so we won't be cold, but if it's wet or windy, we could have it in the conservatory, here at the house, instead. What do you think?"

Mrs Fairbrother graciously approved the fallback plan. More importantly, she promised to ring up all her cronies and tell them about the splendid ladies' programme that she had persuaded Lucy to put on. She was sure they would all attend. They wouldn't want to miss all Mrs Fairbrother's delights.

Lucy said all the correct, polite things and allowed Mrs Fairbrother to purr to the end of the conversation in her own time. Only once she'd ended the call did Lucy allow herself a crow of triumphant laughter. "And this time," she said to her mother's portrait, "I don't even have to ring round all the others. Result!"

It was almost dark when Lucy remembered the one thing she'd failed to do.

Mrs Fairbrother's big idea was a picnic in the arboretum. Unfortunately, under the terms of Gabe's lease, it was now *his* arboretum and Lucy had agreed to the idea without asking him first. It wasn't that he would refuse—at least, she didn't think he would. But Gabe had decided, for reasons Lucy couldn't fathom, that she and her father were "the bosses", while he was just an underling who should do as he was told. If he discovered she'd made a decision about his land without consulting him, it would confirm all his stupid prejudices and he would retreat even further into his shell. She reached for the phone.

"No, I'm not that much of a coward," she said, putting the receiver down again and jumping up from her chair. "You always taught me to face down my demons, Mum, so I will. And anyway, Gabe isn't a demon. He's a…a…"

What was he? She wasn't really sure. He had been a friend, and a good one—or so she had thought—but now he refused to be more than a business acquaintance. Lucy knew she wasn't prepared to settle for that. There had been a time, not long after Gabe graduated from horticultural college, when she'd thought their friendship might blossom into something more. She'd wanted it to. She'd hoped. But then Gabe had found a gardener's job on a big estate on the other side of the country. And within a couple of weeks he was gone. He hadn't written or phoned or emailed. Nothing. And he never visited. Since both his parents were dead, he probably felt he had no one to come back for. Lucy clearly didn't count. Which hurt, though she'd got over it. Eventually.

She'd used the intervening years to learn more about the antiques business and how to mastermind shooting and hunting events for the idle rich. In the end, she'd become so good at it that her father stopped taking any active part in that side of the business. Lucy Cairns had become a success in her own right and she was proud of herself. She even spoke at conferences about the skills of event management.

But she was doing it, essentially, alone. And, deep

down, she didn't want that.

She told herself that she hadn't been carrying a torch for Gabriel Bliss. Not really. But she had to admit that none of her other boyfriends had lasted very long or meant very much to her. They had been pleasant interludes, mostly, but nothing more. Yet, every time she talked to Gabe, or watched the play of his muscles while he planted his beloved trees, or simply saw the way his chocolate eyes lit up with mirth at some silly joke, she felt that old familiar pull.

"Pity the pull only goes in one direction," she snorted, making for the door and Maisie. Whatever had happened to Gabe during his years away, it had certainly changed him. These days he kept his distance from her. And from her father, too, so it wasn't just a male-female thing. Gabe seemed to have become class-conscious, and wealth-conscious, in a way he had never been before. He appeared to hate "the bosses", as he called them. Something must have happened during those years away, something that had warped him. And since he flatly refused to say a word about his time as an estate gardener, Lucy was never going to find out what it was.

The Gabe who'd returned was different. He'd sworn he would never work as a gardener for anyone else. Never again. He would have only one boss—himself.

Lucy was going to have to do her best to deal with Gabe Bliss as he was. And find a way of thawing the thick Bliss permafrost.

How? She hadn't a clue.

Gabe wasn't at the farmshop or anywhere within sight of it.

Muffin was there, though, rushing around her feet and threatening to trip her up. Lucy knelt down to give him a quick cuddle and he responded with a woof and a lick. He was special, even though he didn't belong to her. Without Lucy, he'd have had to be put down after the road accident that led to the loss of his leg, because poor Jane couldn't afford the enormous vet's bills to sort out the mess the poor chap was in. Lucy loved him too much to let him go, she'd said, and so she was more than willing to pay for Muffin's treatment. In the end, Jane had had to swallow her pride and agree, because she didn't want to lose the little dog, either.

Jane welcomed Lucy with a big hug and a warm smile. "I'm not sure where he is, to be honest, lovey. But I'll let him know you were here as soon as he comes in. Urgent, is it? I can get him to give you a ring, if you tell me what it's about."

Oh dear. Jane's nose for information was twitching, as usual. Lucy had been caught that way before. Jane always meant well, but she could be a bit blunt when she was relaying messages. And she was quite capable of passing her news to half the village in the space of an afternoon. This particular bit of business needed to be handled diplomatically—and with an apology—because Lucy was, technically, in the wrong. And had been, from the outset. So Gabe must be the first to hear about it.

"Has he got his mobile with him, do you know, Jane? If he tells me where he's working, I can go and find him."

Jane produced a mobile phone from under the counter and waved it in the air. "No chance. He never takes it with him. Says it's a waste of pocket space because there's never a decent signal. He's right, too."

"Oh, well, never mind." Lucy shrugged. "Another time. I'll just pick up a few goodies while I'm here and then I'll get back to the house." She started round the

21

shelves, picking up goods more or less at random, but always the most expensive. By the time she got back to the checkout, she had a full basket. "These ginger biscuits look fabulous but there was only one packet left. Will you be getting more in, Jane?"

"Er, no. Don't think so." Jane looked a bit sheepish.

"Pity. Never mind. I'm sure you'll have something else to tempt me instead. You always have a lovely selection of stuff." She waited patiently while Jane rang up all the items. Then she paid in cash, as she always did. No point in making Gabe pay several percent to a credit card company when cash could contribute more to his profits. Luckily Gabe was rarely around when Lucy shopped there, so he hadn't had much of a chance to twig what she was up to. So far.

"Thanks a lot, Jane. I'm not in a rush to get back to the house, so I'll take Maisie down the lane by the plantation. You never know, I might see Gabe there. He's bound to come across if I hoot the horn."

She finished packing her purchases into her linen bag and turned to go. "But if I don't manage to catch him, can you ask him to ring me when he has a moment?" she asked, pulling open the shop door. "I'll be in all evening." With a quick pat for Muffin, she nipped out and closed the door behind her before Jane could ask any more questions.

It took several minutes to drive to the plantation lane. Even with a Land Rover, the going was tricky. There had been a lot of rain and there was thick mud everywhere. Still, at least the weather seemed to be clearing, finally. The forecast for the shoot days was pretty good. Of course, if it rained on the picnic day, the ladies wouldn't have to trespass on Gabe's precious arboretum, but Lucy couldn't count on that to get her out of today's embarrassing conversation with him. She had presumed on his good nature and she was probably going to have to grovel a bit to get the consent she needed.

Ah well. In for a penny...

That was when she saw him, at the furthest corner of the plantation. He was planting more bare-root whips. She stopped and turned Maisie's engine off so that she could watch—and admire—without attracting his attention. Gabe had a good rhythm going—pushing the spade into the soil, widening the hole into a V-shape for the root, tucking in the whip and finally firming the soil around it with his heavy boot. It seemed to take only seconds for each of the tiny trees. He could probably plant hundreds, maybe thousands, in a day.

And he'd probably need a long hot soak afterwards, to get rid of the aches and pains.

But it was what Gabe Bliss wanted to do. And he answered to no one but himself while he did it.

Lucy took a deep breath, started Maisie's engine and drove further down the lane until she could stop directly opposite where Gabe was working. Now for it. She turned off the engine and put her hand on the horn.

Someone was leaning on a car horn.

Gabe pushed his spade further into the soil and turned to see what was happening. Was someone in trouble, maybe?

He recognised the old Land Rover. It was probably Lucy, though he was too far away to be sure. He quickly wrapped the sacking round the bundle of whips and began to lope across the field to find out what was up. If it was Lucy, it must be important or she wouldn't have come all the way out here to find him. And if it was one of the other people from the big house, it probably meant something bad. Had Lucy had an accident, maybe?

He began to run faster. But when he saw that it actually was Lucy behind the wheel, he slowed down again. No point in seeming eager to see her.

Even though he was.

When he was about ten yards away, she opened the driver's door and stepped out. But her back foot slipped in the mud and she went down on her bottom, with a gasp of shock. A second later, she was swearing loudly. Then she tried to get up again, using the door mirror for purchase.

"Don't do that," Gabe shouted, lunging to help her. "It'll probably come off in your hand."

Bless her, she laughed. From her ridiculous position, crumpled in an ungainly heap among the mud and the sodden grass, she laughed up into his eyes.

He wanted to kiss her.

"You idiot." He forced himself to frown down at her. "What on earth are you doing out here in *those* shoes?"

Lucy glanced down at her fashionable shoes, which were probably now ruined by the mud, and then looked back up at Gabe. "I was intending to get my wellies out of the back, actually," she said, with surprising dignity. "Unfortunately, the mud got me first." Then the dignity deserted her and she lapsed into giggles. "OK, you win, Gabe. I'm an idiot. Help me up, will you?" She held out a hand.

Which Gabe ignored.

Instead, he took a deep breath, grabbed her by the upper arms and hauled her to her feet. "Don't move," he ordered, "or you'll probably go down again. Let me help you back onto the car seat." He managed to do so without touching any bare skin. "Right. I'll get your wellies. In the back, are they?"

"Actually, I don't need them now. I came to talk to you. And now you're here, I don't need to do any wellie-wading. You do an excellent line in mud, you know."

Gabe grinned. He couldn't help himself. "At least it gets the young trees off to a good start. But that's not what you came to talk about, is it? What can I do for you, Miss Cairns?"

For a moment, Gabe fancied that she was grinding her teeth but all she said was, "I've come to ask you a favour. And to make you an apology."

"Apology?" he asked suspiciously. "Why, what have you done?" In the back of his mind, he added "this time". As a teenager, Lucy was always getting into scrapes. And having to apologise to her elders and betters afterwards. But Gabe wasn't one of her "betters". He was a bit older than Lucy, sure, but she was the boss-lady around here. He wasn't about to forget it, either.

She smiled up at him and shrugged, rather guiltily, he thought. "I've got a very difficult set of wives coming to next week's shoot. So I've been doing a bit of advance placating, because we need them to be there. It's usually the wives who choose the antiques, though it's the husbands who pay, of course."

"And you placated them *how*, exactly?" What had she done that could possibly affect Gabe? If she'd promised that he'd take part in some fancy event for a load of trophy wives without two brain cells to rub together, he would probably wring Lucy's neck. He could feel the tide of anger rising already.

"I, er, I told them they could have an al fresco lunch in the arboretum. Your arboretum." She was blushing now. "I'm really sorry, Gabe. I should have cleared it with you first, but the damn woman was so insistent that I forgot about the legal niceties. And so I—"

Gabe laughed with relief. And all his anger evaporated on the spot. "Is that all? I was expecting something much, much worse." He made a face at her. "Besides, I only lease the land from your father. It is still *his* arboretum, really. I can't very well deny you access. Especially for such a harmless event."

"That's kind of you, Gabe, but I think you're wrong. Legally, you're entitled to the quiet enjoyment of the land you lease from us. I don't think we do have the right to enter without your permission."

Gabe had known that perfectly well—he'd studied his lease with care and taken legal advice before he signed—but he hadn't expected Lucy to be so well up in the law. Another case of underestimating the shrewd brain under those enticing blonde curls.

He took a deep breath. Then another. "Miss Cairns, you and your clients may picnic in the arboretum with my goodwill. I hope the sun shines on you. It's only October, after all, so you might be in luck."

"Oh, Gabe, that's so kind of you. I'll make sure they're careful, I promise."

Careful? Oh. Yes, of course. He'd forgotten that some of her rich clients did unpredictable things, especially when they'd had a few glasses too many.

"But I'm relying on you, Miss Cairns, to make sure none of them harms any of the trees. If they do, I'm afraid I'll be looking to you to make good the damage." He shrugged. "Sorry, but there's nothing else I can do."

"Seems eminently fair," Lucy said. "And I'll make sure the gas heaters are sited well away from any of the trees."

"*Gas heaters?*" He could see catastrophe looming already. Pampered trophy wives were capable of anything. It wouldn't be only broken branches. Whole trees might go up in smoke. In that instant, he had the smell of burning pine in his nostrils and righteous fury in his veins. "Are you *actually* going to put gas heaters among my trees?"

She sighed. "I have to, I'm afraid. Otherwise the tender wifely flowers might wilt in the cold. But I promise I won't let them damage anything. If I think there's a risk of that, I'll cart them all off back to the conservatory."

"I'll hold you to that." He was trying not to let his irritation show and not quite succeeding. He knew he shouldn't take it out on her. She was sensible and practical. She'd probably have industrial-sized fire extinguishers behind every tree and the fire brigade on speed dial. And she would marshal her clients so tactfully they would never know what had hit them. His trees should be perfectly safe with Lucy.

But there was always that one in a million chance…

If he stayed talking to her, he might say something he would regret. "Now I've got to get back to my planting, so if you'll excuse me…" He turned his back before she could say another word. Then he stomped across the mud to his whips. They at least were easy to handle.

# Chapter Three

MRS FAIRBROTHER WAS pontificating, waving her champagne flute in the vague direction of some of Gabe's conifers. "Lucy and I chose an excellent spot for a picnic, I'd say, even in October." She smiled round at the other wives and girlfriends. "But I knew I was right to insist on heaters. We'd have been freezing out here without them."

Lucy plastered her best company smile on her face and continued to hand round the dainty canapés that formed the first course. For dinner parties in the big house, she always employed some of the locals as waiters and waitresses—the guests expected so see Sir Andrew at the head of the long mahogany table and Lucy, his co-host, at the opposite end—but Mrs Fairbrother had insisted on informality for the ladies' picnic. "Just us gels together," she'd said. Of course, there was a limit to her informality. There still had to be a proper table and chairs, with starched white napkins, silver cutlery and all the rest of the paraphernalia the guests were used to. Informality simply meant that Lucy was having to be both host and butler at the same time. Guests like these were unlikely ever to think of lifting a finger to help.

To be fair, they'd paid so much money for the shoot— or rather, their husbands had—that it would have been unreasonable to expect them to help with the serving, or with anything else. Lucy warned herself to remain on her best behaviour and to remember this was business. She should focus on the antiques she had already sold and the other sales to come. Perhaps she should even inflate her prices a bit for these women, as a sort of gratuity for her waitressing efforts? She could give the extra profit to the local food bank where it would do good in a way these women would never understand. Yes, she'd do that. Serve them right. Not that they'd ever notice, anyway. They didn't seem to notice much at all. Here they were, among Gabe's towering trees—some gold, some blue, some frothy green—and not one of the women had let slip a single word about the beauty of the landscape around them or reached out to stroke a delicate branch. How could they miss all that natural grandeur? It made no sense.

"More champagne?" she murmured dutifully, retrieving the napkin-covered bottle from the side table where the food was laid out.

All but one of the ladies held out their flutes. Lucy poured until her bottle was empty. Then she fetched another bottle from the cool box, opened it without spilling a drop, and began to refill the remaining glasses.

"Gawd." Tina, by far the youngest of the women, was fluttering her false eyelashes. "How'd you do that? Whenever I open champagne, it goes all over everywhere. Spraying, y'know? Sort of like they do at those motor racing thingies." She made a face. "Graham got ever so cross with me last time. Because it was *Cristal*, prob'ly. Made me promise I'd let a man do it in future."

Poor kid, Lucy thought. The joys of being a trophy wife, eh? "It's a simple trick once you know how to do it," she explained patiently. "After you've taken off the foil and the wire, you hold the cork with a napkin and then you turn the bottle, not the cork. Slowly and gently. The cork eases out with a gentle pop. Usually."

Tina looked impressed and disbelieving at the same time.

"Would you like to have a go with the next bottle?" Lucy offered. "This one's almost empty." Tina was not very bright, perhaps, but she was very sweet and didn't deserve to be treated like a dimwit. It wasn't only her husband who patronised her, either. The other women looked down on her, too, and Lucy wasn't prepared to put up with that.

"Ooh, yeah. That'd be mega." Tina jumped to her feet and reached out to grab a fresh bottle from the cool box.

Lucy caught her arm just in time. The last thing she wanted was Tina spraying champagne all over the other guests. "Gently. It's really important not to shake the bottle when you're opening it. And of course it needs to be properly cold. Warm champagne always froths up."

"Warm champagne. Ugh," put in Mrs Fairbrother, with a grimace. "I sacked a butler for serving the champagne too warm, only last year. It was ghastly."

Ghastly for the sacked butler, too, Lucy thought, especially if he had to leave without a reference. Pretending she hadn't heard, Lucy concentrated instead on helping Tina to open her bottle. The cork popped out with relative ease and there was only the tiniest amount of spillage. "Well done," Lucy said, with a conspiratorial grin. "For a first time, that was brilliant."

Tina was blushing. But she was triumphant, too. "I'll pour," she announced. "Since I opened it, I should buttle. If I practise, I can show Graham I'm not such a wuss after all."

"Your husband will be proud of you, I'm sure," Lucy said kindly. "And while you're doing that, I can fetch the next course."

Lucy loaded a tray with salads, baked potatoes, bread, butter and condiments. The gas-fired chafing dishes would remain on the side table for the ladies to help themselves. This time, they'd actually have to get up to fill their own plates. Such a hardship for the little darlings.

Lucy set the food out on the damask cloth and began to clear away the uneaten canapés and the used plates from the first course.

"If you'd like to help yourselves, ladies?" She waved in the direction of the side table. "There are hot plates beside the chafing dishes. There's a choice of *coq au vin* or salmon in a Riesling and cream sauce. There's herby rice for anyone who'd like it. And I have red Burgundy or Riesling for anyone who doesn't want to drink champagne with the food."

"Red wine with chicken? Surely not." Mrs Sinclair made a face and then tossed off the rest of her champagne.

Ah. Time for tact. It was important not to make Mrs Sinclair look as unsophisticated as she clearly was. "Since our chef makes the *coq au vin* with fine red Burgundy, he recommends drinking the same wine. 'One bottle of Chambertin in the dish, one bottle on the table,' is his motto. He's Belgian rather than French, of course, so we have to make allowances," Lucy added with a laugh.

It seemed to work. Mrs Sinclair laughed too and did not look embarrassed. "Poirot used to have that problem, didn't he? People thinking he was French when he wasn't. He used to get quite uppity about it, I remember."

It sounded as though Mrs Sinclair thought Poirot was a real person. "David Suchet plays Poirot brilliantly, I agree," Lucy said. "Some other actors try to turn him into a caricature."

"How right you are," Mrs Fairbrother put in. "In that famous film—the one with the train—the lead actor was totally OTT, I thought. Not Suchet. The other one. Can't remember his name offhand, but he's quite famous."

No one responded, apparently because no one was listening. They were all crowding round the chafing dishes, filling their plates. Lucy was constantly surprised by how much the trophy wives ate and drank, considering how stick thin they all were. Perhaps they starved themselves when they went back home? Or perhaps they did worse things to ensure they didn't absorb the calories they poured down their throats? Lucy didn't like to think about what those worse things might be.

"Lucy, might I try some of the Chambertin with this chicken?" Mrs Sinclair asked. "The red wine sauce smells delicious so I thought I should follow your chef's advice. Even if he is Belgian." She tittered at her own joke. But she'd taken the point about *coq au vin* and red wine, so maybe she was more on the ball than Lucy had thought.

"Of course. I'll fetch the decanter." Lucy went round to the other side of the huge conifer where the wine and her spare supplies were waiting.

And found she wasn't alone.

Gabe was standing there with his hands on his hips. And he was frowning.

"What are you doing here, Gabe?" Lucy hissed. "My guests won't like it if they think they're being spied on. Especially by a bloke. This is supposed to be an informal girls' lunch, you know."

Gabe looked down at the ample supplies resting against his tree. "Informal, my foot. Looks like the sort of thing Princess Margaret used to do."

"Not quite," Lucy replied tartly. "Princess Margaret used to have a bevy of servants in tow. Probably silver candlesticks as well."

"Whereas this posse of pampered princesses doesn't need servants. They have you, instead, don't they?"

He'd made no attempt to hide the sarcasm in his tone. Predictable, of course, given his views about class. But he'd known exactly what kind of women she'd be entertaining in his beloved arboretum, so why had he risked contamination by coming anywhere near? And why did he care if Lucy was waiting on them? Did that mean—?

She didn't have time to unravel how Gabe's mind worked. What mattered was to prevent a scene. "Keep your voice down. They'll hear you." The last thing she needed was for him to upset her guests. Especially as he was looking particularly filthy and sweaty today. His T-shirt was stained and sticking to his skin. His hands were caked in dirt. What on earth had he been doing all morning? Digging a ditch? "And if they see you," she added, narrowing her eyes as even more of his dirt registered, "they'll probably run a mile, thinking you're some kind of filthy vagabond, out to rob them."

He grinned, but Lucy didn't think he was amused. It

looked more like a feral snarl, his teeth very white in his tanned and soil-streaked face.

In an attempt to make him leave, she said the first thing that came into her mind. "That grin makes you look like the Big Bad Wolf." He did, too. Dark, and very dangerous. "But Red Riding Hood isn't available today so you'll have to take your appetites somewhere else." Uh-oh, bad image. And too late to take it back. In desperation, she made shooing motions at him, which he ignored.

He simply shook his head at her. "Funnily enough, I do have an appetite. And my arboretum is overflowing with food, too." Now he was mocking her, getting his own back for that stupid Big Bad Wolf jibe. "You'd think someone could spare a few leftovers for a hungry worker."

"Hungry worker? What is this...this *person* doing here, Lucy?" Mrs Fairbrother had appeared and was looking down her nose at Gabe.

Before Lucy could say a word, Tina arrived to find out what was going on. Unlike Mrs Fairbrother, Tina was young enough to appreciate a honed male body. Her eyes widened as she clocked Gabe. Yes, he was filthy and sweaty, but it was the result of good honest toil and the stained T-shirt was clinging in all the right places. Lucy suspected Tina was counting Gabe's abs. She found herself doing the same.

"Come back to the table, Tina," Mrs Fairbrother ordered, taking the younger woman by the arm to pull her away. "You, too, Lucy. There's no need to wait on us any more. We'll all serve ourselves. It'll be fun to pretend we're plebs, won't it?" She glanced at Gabe again and screwed up her nose. "Though I wouldn't like to be quite as dirty as your gardener, or whatever he is. Certainly not fit for the company of ladies."

"Mrs Fairbrother, this is—" But before Lucy could finish her sentence, Mrs Fairbrother and Tina had gone. Beside her, Gabe was white to the gills. Lucy thought he had clenched his teeth, too. Unfortunately for her, he had cause.

Lucy tried to put a hand on his arm but he shook her off. "Don't touch me. I'm filthy, remember? Not fit for the company of ladies like you."

"Gabe, I—"

"I'll be off out of your way. I only wanted to check on those heaters of yours. Two of them—" he pointed to the offending contraptions "—are very close to the trees, so don't turn them up any higher. I don't want my trees to get burnt." He marched off before Lucy could reply. With luck, he failed to hear what she muttered at his retreating back.

*I'll give her Big Bad Wolf. If she knew what my real appetites were, she'd run a mile, instead of standing there, trying to shoo me away like a stroppy hen.*

Gabe kicked a tree stump. Hard. Even his heavy boots made no impression at all. He muttered an apology—it wasn't the tree stump's fault that he was in a foul temper—and went to retrieve his spade.

The truth was that he didn't like to see Lucy waiting hand and foot on women like those. And that Fairbrother woman was a bullying old harridan. As toffee-nosed and arrogant in her way as the man who had fired Gabe over the rhododendron. *Not fit for the company of ladies,* indeed. How dare she? There was nothing wrong with a bit of honest sweat and dirt. At least Gabe was working for his money. What had Mrs Fairbrother ever done for hers?

The answer was so obvious—and so crudely vivid in his imagination—that he laughed out loud. Sometimes, he thought with a sigh, he could be his own worst enemy. He really shouldn't let himself get worked up when it came to Lucy Cairns. She didn't need any help from him. She was quite capable of looking after herself.

And he could trust her to look after his trees, too.

Sighing, and frustrated, Lucy returned to the table with the decanter of red wine and the chilled Riesling. All the ladies were eating greedily—Lucy's chef always produced fabulous food, worthy of the fabulous fees she paid him—and, for this course, they expected Lucy to join them. She made sure all the glasses were filled before she sat down, though. And she took only a very small portion of the fish. She would need to eat quickly so that she could serve more wine, clear the plates and then serve dessert. She doubted that her "pretend plebs" would want to do that for themselves, whatever Mrs Fairbrother said.

"The wind's getting up a bit," Mrs Sinclair said, between mouthfuls. "Can we move one of these heaters a bit closer? I'm getting cold."

Oh dear. Lucy knew better than to move the gas heaters over uneven ground while they were running. There might be an accident. "I can't move them without help, I'm afraid," she began.

"Can't you summon that labouring fellow to do it?" Mrs Fairbrother demanded.

"Sorry, he's gone back to work. There's only me."

"Oh. Well, couldn't you turn the heaters up a bit? This one here—" she gestured to the one between her and a rare blue spruce "—doesn't seem to be producing much heat at all. And I'm getting really cold."

"I can't turn that one up any higher without risking damage to the tree," Lucy explained, making a gesture of helplessness. "All the trees here in the arboretum are specimens, you see, and some of them are very rare."

"Nonsense. It's only a tree." Before Lucy could do anything, Mrs Fairbrother sprang up from her chair and turned the heater up to maximum.

The smell of burning resin hit Lucy's nostrils in seconds. She jumped up so quickly, she knocked her chair over. Sprinting round the table, she turned the heater off altogether. Then she examined the branch nearest the heater. There was a small amount of damage but she'd prevented anything really bad, thank goodness. She'd have to own up to Gabe though, and pay up, too. In more ways than one. She was bound to get the sharp end of his tongue. But that would come later. Her guests had to come first. She took a deep breath and turned back to them.

Mrs Fairbrother was seething. "What on earth are you doing, Lucy? I said I was cold."

"Yes, and I'm sorry, Mrs Fairbrother, but the heater was burning the tree." She swallowed hard and grabbed for the first excuse she could think of. "I daren't risk a fire. Conifers catch fire very quickly, you see—it's all that resin—and a spark could have set light to the tablecloth. Or even someone's clothes."

Tina made a sound that was somewhere between a gasp and a shriek.

Lucy smiled placatingly at her would-be nemesis. "Why don't you change places with me, Mrs Fairbrother?" She gestured to the heater near her fallen chair. "I can turn that heater up full so you'll soon be toasty warm again."

Mrs Fairbrother grudgingly accepted and Lucy fussed

around her, settling the woman in her new place with a thick rug and making sure the heater was turned up to maximum. "Let me fetch you another plate of *coq au vin*. This one's gone cold. Would you like a fresh glass of wine, too?"

Lucy braved the nursery next morning as soon as all her guests had left. She didn't want Gabe to discover the damage for himself. She had to be the one to tell him. So she took him to the arboretum and showed him.

Predictably, he went up like a rocket. "I *told* you," he raged, wagging his finger so close to Lucy's face it almost poked her in the eye. "And I *trusted* you. Are you so stupid you—"

"I am *not* stupid. And I'll thank you to remember it, Gabriel Bliss," she cut in firmly, trying to keep the anger out of her voice. Even though she was in the wrong, Lucy was not going to put up with that sort of insult. Not from him. Some of her guests might be a bit uncaring— sometimes more than a bit—but Gabe was overreacting, big time. Typical. "I've told you I'll pay for the damage. And there isn't very much—even you have to admit that. You can trim that scorched branch, can't you? Or cut it back to the trunk, if you have to?"

"It's not that," he muttered crossly. But at least he'd stopped yelling at her. "It didn't have to happen at all. It's not as if I didn't warn you, is it?"

*And it wasn't my doing.* The thought popped into Lucy's head, but she didn't say it out loud. Her business. Her responsibility if her clients damaged anything. Her shoulders were broad. She would take the blame. *And* bite her tongue. Well, a bit. "Yes, Gabe, you did warn me. And, as I said, I'm really sorry the spruce got scorched." In fact, she'd been so angry with Mrs High-

and-Mighty Fairbrother that she'd wanted to give the woman a piece of her mind. That was impossible, of course, so she'd got her own back in the only way she could—by doubling the price of the silk rug the woman had taken a fancy to. With luck, the extra profit would pay for the damage in the arboretum with a fair chunk left over for the food bank.

Lucy sighed loudly. Even Gabe couldn't ignore that. "It's unfortunate, but accidents do happen. So now I have to make amends. And I will. How much would it cost to replace the tree?"

Gabe's eyes widened. "Replace it? You're kidding." When Lucy shook her head, he said, sounding slightly dazed, "I…I doubt it would be possible to replace it, like for like. Well-grown specimens of this age are very rare and hard to source."

"Er… You mean they don't grow on trees?" she quipped.

He gave a gasp of laughter, tried to look affronted, and failed. A second later, he laughed again, a real laugh this time. They were sharing a stupid joke, as they had done so often when they were kids together. It made Lucy realise how much she had missed their camaraderie.

He wagged his finger at her again, but now he was grinning and there was even a twinkle in his eye. He was in pantomime mode. "You are a very wicked woman, Lucy Cairns. Has anyone ever told you that?"

"Possibly," she replied, twinkling back at him. She'd be able to make amends now. Inwardly, she was glowing, but she knew better than to let him see that. She was still the landlord's daughter. So this had to be all business. "OK, here's my offer. If I pay you the full price of a replacement tree and you do whatever repairs are necessary to make this one look pristine again, can we call it quits?"

He protested a bit. If he took the full price of the tree, he maintained, he ought to be replacing it, not just doing a bit of remedial pruning.

In Lucy's opinion, Gabe was sometimes too straight for his own good. But then, maybe that was why she—

*Don't go there. Keep on the practical stuff.*

She was pretty sure she'd win in the end, but she was going to have to be very, very tactful. They argued for a while, but good-naturedly. Eventually, they reached a compromise, at around half the price of a replacement tree, and solemnly shook hands on their deal.

Wonder of wonders, Gabe was still smiling as she strode off to retrieve Maisie and drive back to the Manor. With the staff and the guests all gone, the big house would be mercifully quiet. Lucy and her dad could rattle around in it all by themselves.

"Male egos, eh, Maisie? Good job I had Dad to practise on before I started on Gabe." Maisie didn't respond. "Talk about diplomacy. Selling an idea to Gabe is like selling ice cream to Eskimos. Worse, possibly." She smiled inwardly. But she hadn't really won. Not on everything. She crossed her fingers on the steering wheel and silently promised herself that she'd find a way of putting part of her excess Fairbrother profit into Gabe's business. Somehow.

Not via fancy biscuits, though.

"I'd burst out of my clothes if I ate that many," she laughed out loud, struck by the comic image of splitting seams and bulging flesh.

Maisie, possibly confused, gave a half-hearted burp from her back end.

## Chapter Four

NOVEMBER WAS TYPICALLY WET, cold and dark.
All the whips had been planted, so there wasn't very
much for Gabe to do after he'd seen to the daily
watering. It was too early to start cutting Christmas trees.
He wouldn't have any customers for them until the start
of December at the earliest. And he prided himself on
always offering freshly felled trees that wouldn't start
dropping their needles the moment they were taken into
a centrally-heated house.

Should he take over from Jane in the shop? Offer her
the afternoon off?

No chance. That was a certain recipe for being sent
off with a flea in his ear.

So…

He remembered something he'd seen in the local
paper. Something interesting. He popped his head round
the shop door and waved to distract Jane from her
reading. Muffin, sensible chap, was curled up in his
basket by the counter. He raised his head and wagged his

tail, but he didn't emerge from his snug cocoon.

"Do you need me for anything this afternoon?" Gabe asked. "I was thinking of going down town. There's something I'd like to do. But if you need me here…"

Jane gestured to the empty shop with her magazine. "To serve all these eager customers, d'you mean, lovey?" They both laughed. November was a very slow month but someone had to be here, just in case. "No, you go and enjoy yourself. You deserve an afternoon off after all the hours you've been putting in. Planning something special, are you?"

He knew the sort of thing she wanted him to do. And it usually involved the opposite sex. Jane was keen to see Gabe hitched to "a nice local lass", as she put it. She was on a loser there. Especially today.

"Actually, there's a really interesting exhibition on at the museum. About how people lived round here a century or more ago. Apparently they've dug out a lot of stuff that's never been on display before. Early photographs and letters. You know the sort of thing."

Jane's dropped jaw suggested she didn't.

"Anyway, that's where I'm going. As long as you don't need me?"

Jane shook her head. Then she smiled broadly. "I'll lock up. See you tomorrow."

For once, Lucy was having trouble with her monthly accounts. It had never happened before. Normally, she whizzed through them. And enjoyed the satisfaction of getting everything to balance and reaching a positive bottom-line figure. But today, the accounts were refusing to play ball.

She sat back in her chair, using two firm fingers to rub away the frown between her eyes, and breathed a long sigh in the direction of the picture above the fireplace. "Not a good day, today, Mum," she said, with resignation. "I don't know why, but nothing feels right, just at the moment."

Something in the picture caught her eye and she sat up, suddenly rigid with shock. The picture was fading!

At least, part of it was.

Could it be a trick of the light?

She jumped up and crossed to the portrait. She peered at it. Then she went to the door to flip the switch for the overhead lights. She went back and peered at the picture again, even more closely. She wasn't seeing things. The portrait, as a whole, seemed to be just as it always way, except...

The wedding ring on her mother's hand had faded so much that it was almost invisible. None of the other yellows and golds in the portrait had faded. Not a bit.

Lucy swore under her breath. What if her father noticed? What if he asked about the ring?

She slumped into the chair by the fireplace and dropped her head into her hands. She'd never told him.

He'd never asked.

But if he did, she'd have to come clean. And he would be devastated.

She took a deep breath and forced herself to stare up at the portrait again. She wasn't mistaken. Her mother's wedding ring was fading out of existence. And it was Lucy's fault.

At that moment—the worst of all possible moments—the door opened and her father came in. "Lucy, I wanted to—" He stopped in his tracks. "Hey, what's the matter? You look as if you'd lost a pound and found a penny." He dropped into the chair opposite her and reached out to pat her arm. "Come on," he said, in the generous way she'd always loved, "you can tell your old dad. No matter what it is."

No, she couldn't. The one taboo between them was anything to do with his dead wife. And the question of the ring would be worse than anything else.

She tried to force a smile. She thought she half-succeeded. "I was trying to do the books for last month and, for some reason or other, I kept getting it wrong." It wasn't the truth, but it wasn't exactly a lie, either.

"Really? Now that does surprise me, given your head for figures." He shook his head. "Ah, I know what it is. You've been working too hard. You need some time off. When was the last time you had a holiday?"

"Well…"

"Yes, precisely. What you need is a break. The business won't fall apart if October's accounts aren't done for a week or two. We're nowhere near the year end, so there's no pressure."

Lucy took a deep breath, glad to have deflected him from the portrait. "You're probably right, Dad. In fact, I'm sure you are. Pat will be here tomorrow and the day after, so I can take a couple of days off." She smiled at him, properly this time, and reached out to stroke his hand. "You're a right old softie, aren't you? I thought you were supposed to be the hard man of business."

He laughed, a genuine honest-to-goodness laugh. "I can be a hard man. Yes. But I like to think I'm an honest one. I stick to my word and I value the people who work for me. And that includes you, Lucy Cairns. I learned a long time ago that if you work good employees too hard, you burn them out. That's not in their interest, or mine. And, since you are who you are, I have even more interest in looking after your well-being. So, let's have less of the 'hard-man' stuff, if you please, and a bit more of the 'softie dad looking after his daughter', hmm?"

Lucy chortled. That was about as much of a statement of love as she'd ever heard from him. And she knew that he had only said it because he was worried about her. "Thanks, Dad. I think you're better at taking care of me than I am at taking care of myself."

He rose, smiling down at her. Then he transferred his gaze to the portrait and his smile vanished. "You're all I have left of her, so it makes all sorts of sense for me to take care of you. I didn't—"

Whatever it was he'd been going to say, he stopped dead.

Lucy froze, not daring to speak. Hardly daring to breathe. She wanted to take away his pain but if she tried to comfort him, she'd make things worse, she knew. She'd tried that in the past; and failed miserably.

The lines round his mouth seemed to deepen as he stood there. The colour had leached out of his face, too. After another minute, he shook his head and walked out.

Lucy sighed. "Sorry, Mum," she said to the portrait. She was sure he'd been about to say that he'd failed her mother and he wasn't going to fail Lucy. "I didn't mean to bring that on. But at least he didn't notice the ring. Or, if he did, he didn't ask about it." She lifted her left hand and gazed at it accusingly. "Just as well. Because there's absolutely nothing I can do to make things right again."

Gabe had been wandering around the exhibits for over an hour. The whole display was fascinating, especially to a history nut like him. There were diaries, and letters, and bits of costume from the nineteenth century—how on earth did women squeeze themselves into those corseted bodices? They weren't kidding when they spoke about handspan waists.

45

He was poring over a commonplace book kept by a middle-class Victorian wife. It was an extraordinary jumble of recipes, remedies for various ills—most of which sounded more dangerous than the diseases they were supposed to cure—personal comments, and pictures and cuttings from newspapers and magazines. Basically, the woman seemed to have copied down anything that struck her as interesting. And it *was* interesting, a century and a half later. How could a woman transcribe a remedy for gout at one minute and a recipe for pickled mushrooms the next?

Alice, the curator, had generously allowed him to take the book out and turn the pages. Most museum staff wouldn't have allowed a visitor to do such a thing. But Alice knew Gabe and his interest in all things historical, so she was trusting him with it while the exhibition was quiet. Provided he put on the white cotton gloves she supplied, of course.

But he'd monopolised the book for long enough. Other visitors had come in and they were entitled to look at it, too.

He carefully turned back to the page that had originally been on display and put the book back into the glass case. Then he went across to the desk, pulling off the cotton gloves. "That was really kind of you, Alice. That commonplace book is utterly fascinating. I've never seen such a mishmash of stuff and yet it shows something of what her life must have been like. Gout, and pickled mushrooms, and the latest news from the colonies. The latest fashions, too."

Alice nodded. "Yes. It's a great resource. We could actually do with someone to catalogue the material that's in that book. Unfortunately, none of the staff has the time to do it. We were hoping that one of the volunteers might take it on. But nobody has offered yet. I don't suppose…?"

Um. Now she'd put him on the spot. But he didn't really have time, what with Christmas coming. "Well, um, I don't think I can volunteer this side of Christmas, but, er, maybe in January? Can I get back to you on that, Alice?"

She smiled in a way that suggested she didn't believe him for a moment. "We'd be very grateful for any time you could spare us, Gabe." That answer was a model of diplomacy and tact. "Whenever suits you."

Oh. "Yes, well— Yes, I'll, er, I'll get back to you."

"By the way," Alice said, responding to Gabe's obvious embarrassment, "have you looked at the section over there by the far wall?" She pointed. Gabe shook his head. "There's some interesting stuff about the Manor House. You know, Sir Andrew Cairns's place? We unearthed an early picture—a daguerreotype, actually— of the Victorian owners. The house looked much the same then as it does now."

"Really? I'll take a look. Daguerreotypes? They're not real photographs, are they?"

"No. They're… Well, they were an early attempt at photography. But the process was totally different. They were very popular in the 1840s and 1850s, before the invention of the kind of photography you and I might recognise. They're really fragile, though, just a film of silver that's been exposed to light to create an image. You can't even remove the glass, because the silver tarnishes if it's exposed to the air.

"Some of the earliest daguerreotypes were lost as a result of overzealous attempts at cleaning by conservators who should have known better." Her disapproval was clear. "Not that long ago, either. Some of Daguerre's originals were destroyed in the seventies."

She led him over to the dimly-lit case in the corner of the exhibition. "It's really quite difficult to see," she said.

"It looks like a negative, not a photograph." He couldn't make it out.

"Ah, that's because you're standing in the wrong place. Daguerreotypes are both negative and positive, depending on how you view them. A bit like the holograms on a credit card, you know? If you stand here, you'll see it as a normal picture." She pulled him towards her. "OK? I'll leave you to it."

Now that Gabe was viewing the image from the right angle, he could see quite well, in spite of the fact that there wasn't much light in this corner. Alice was right. The house looked pretty much the same, except that there seemed to be a profusion of flowering plants in beds around the front door. The Victorian owners probably had dozens of gardeners. Nowadays, there was topiary in huge pots on either side of the front door and nothing else. Nowadays, gardeners were expensive (but disposable).

Gabe looked more closely, not at the flowers, but at the couple standing in the centre of the image. It was difficult to judge the period from the man's clothes, but the woman's gown might well have been from the 1840s. It was nothing like the vast crinolines of later in the century. She had light-coloured hair, in ringlets, and a very pretty face. In fact, she—

He bent down to peer more closely. She looked just like Lucy. With a Victorian hairdo. How odd.

Then he looked—really looked—at the man. He was tall, with dark hair, and impressive side-whiskers.

And he looked almost exactly like Gabe.

Gabe was so shocked that, for a moment, he froze. It

was a picture of him. And Lucy. Master and mistress of the Manor House. But it couldn't be!

He shook his head to clear it. But the image didn't change. The pair weren't smiling, of course, but they looked really comfortable together. As if they shared a deep understanding. The kind of understanding that came from a love match...

He couldn't go there! He had to be purely practical about this. He checked the caption below the daguerreotype. No names. The date was thought to be mid-1840s. The couple was believed to be the owner of the Manor House and his wife.

*I don't believe this. I couldn't have had a double who was a landowner. Not even a couple of centuries ago. My family aren't descended from landowners. If we were anything, we were landless peasants, and illiterate ones, at that.*

But the evidence of the image seemed so strong. Gabe. And Lucy. Man and wife?

He was losing his grip. He pulled his phone out of his pocket. He had to have a record of this. He needed to study it more closely. In detail. But on his own. Not in a public place like this.

He tried to focus the camera, but it was difficult. There was so little light. If he got the angle wrong, he'd get the negative rather than the positive image.

"Gabe." Alice was back, putting a firm, restraining hand on his arm. "I'm sorry, you can't do that." She pointed to the sign on the wall: a camera with a vivid red line through it. "Even without flash. I'm sorry. It's against the rules."

"Oh. I beg your pardon, Alice, I didn't mean to— I didn't— Sorry, I—" He stuffed his phone back into his pocket. "It's just that this picture— Sorry, never mind."

He told himself to stop gabbling like an idiot. That was a sure-fire way to rouse Alice's curiosity about what was getting to him. And if she looked closely at that image, she'd be bound to see the likeness and start asking awkward questions. Questions even he didn't know the answer to. Time to go.

"Thank you for all your help today, Alice. I...I need to go now. I need to get back to the nursery. Jane will be wanting to lock up and get home. See you again." And then, knowing he was probably red to the roots of his hair, he fled.

In the days that followed, Gabe couldn't stop thinking about that image. Him— Gabriel Bliss—married to Lucy Cairns. And the plutocratic owner of a grand mansion as well. Employer of zillions of servants, probably all underpaid and overworked.

It was impossible. All of it. He must have been seeing things. A woman like Lucy was not for him.

He told himself he could go back to the museum and have another look at that weird image. Maybe, he'd been mistaken? Maybe, it wasn't his doppelgänger after all? Perhaps he could ask Alice's opinion?

But he was much too busy to take another day off.

That's what he told himself.

And by the time he'd worked up the courage to contemplate another visit, the exhibition was over. The daguerreotype would be back in the vaults and Alice might have some very awkward questions if he asked her to get it out for him. So his decision was made for him.

He heaved a sigh of relief and went back to his trees. Whatever he'd thought he'd seen, it didn't matter. He had his Christmas customers to focus on. And his potted trees. Nothing else mattered.

# Chapter Five

THE WIND WAS WHISTLING round and howling like a banshee. In spite of all the money Lucy's father had spent on renovations, the old house was creaking and groaning under the onslaught of the gale. She glanced out of the window. It was already dark outside. Well, what did she expect in December? It would be the shortest day, pretty soon. And winter gales were par for the course at this time of year.

She checked her watch. It was well after four. There was unlikely to be any more business today so perhaps she could pack up early?

She went across to the fireplace. There was only a small amount of wood still burning in the stove. It would be out in an hour or so. With the door of the log burner safely closed, there was no problem about leaving the fire to die down.

She gathered up the papers she had been working on—they could certainly wait until the next day—and put them away. Desk clear, she made for the door.

And then the phone rang.

*Damn and blast!* Should she let it go to the answering machine?

No, she couldn't do that. She was a professional. Professionals dealt with business when it arrived. She went back to her desk and picked up the phone. "Cairns Antiques. Lucy Cairns speaking."

"Lucy. Oh, thank God." It was Jane. And she sounded really stressed.

"What is it, Jane? Has something happened?"

"I don't know. Maybe. Lucy, I didn't— I'm sorry, I didn't know who else to call. I'm in the shop on my own and I can't leave."

"What's the matter? What's happened?"

"It's Gabe. Or... maybe it's Gabe. He promised he'd be back by three so that I could get off early. I've got to sort the costumes for the Nativity Play and— Anyway, that doesn't matter. The point is—" Lucy could hear Jane's anxious breathing, getting shorter and louder all the time "—it's well after four and he hasn't come back. He never breaks his promises and, with this awful weather, I..."

"Where has he gone?"

"I think he went to the arboretum. He was worried about some of the trees in this awful wind. And... Oh, I don't know, but I had this feeling..."

Lucy shivered. Now she had the feeling, too. But she must do everything possible to reassure Jane. "Don't worry, Jane. You stay where you are. I'll go to the arboretum and find out what's going on. He's probably been shoring up trees and lost track of time. I'll tell him to expect a piece of your mind, shall I?"

"Oh, Lucy. You're a star."

"When I find him, I'll bring him back to the shop and

you can give him a real bollocking. And you'll be able to get off to the school, too. With luck, you won't be too late for the costume fitting."

Jane started to thank Lucy again, but Lucy wasn't having any of it. "No need for that. I've got to get off. It's getting darker, and wetter, by the minute. See you soon." Lucy put the phone down and raced for the hall, her raincoat, and the redoubtable Maisie. In this weather, nothing less than a four-by-four would do.

When Lucy reached the entrance to the arboretum, one glance told her what had happened. The ancient and beautiful blue cedar had dropped an enormous branch. Even from a distance and through the rain, she could see the pale wound on the trunk. But Gabe would have known that cedars were prone to breaking. Even Lucy knew they were dangerous. So he wouldn't have gone near it in the middle of a thundering gale, surely?

Maybe he was trying to save the tree from further damage? Maybe he was OK and still working on it, forgetting his promise to Jane?

Lucy had to know. She banged Maisie into four-wheel drive and raced her across the sodden grass.

She found Gabe lying on the ground next to a huge cedar branch. Eyes closed. Unconscious. How long had he been out for?

Lucy pulled out her phone. *No signal. Not even for emergencies. Damn, damn, damn!* She'd have to go back to the farmshop to call the ambulance.

*But I shouldn't leave him.*

She would have to leave him.

Remembering her first-aid training, she checked that he was breathing and that his airways were clear. His pulse was pretty strong, but erratic. Should she put him

53

in the recovery position?

No. No, she mustn't move him. His spine might have been damaged when the cedar bough struck him. It was massive enough to break bones. All she could do was to try to keep him warm and dry. And then run for help.

She ripped off her raincoat and tucked it over and round him. At least it was long enough to cover most of his body and keep him from getting any wetter.

"Oh, Gabe." She touched her hand to his cold cheek. His skin was ashen, almost blue, under his tan. "You probably can't hear me, but I'll be back very soon. I promise. I'm going to get help." She jumped to her feet, without stopping to brush the wet soil off the knees of her trousers, and sprinted for Maisie. Inside, she checked her phone once more as she turned the key in the ignition. Still no signal. Predictable. No point in checking again on the way back. Besides, she needed human help. And the only person around to provide it was Jane. She gunned the engine and raced old Maisie across the grass towards the road and the haven of the shop.

She screeched to a halt when she reached her goal. Jumping out, she saw that she did have a phone signal at last. She was already dialling the emergency services as she raced for the door. If Jane heard her reporting what had happened, Lucy wouldn't have to repeat herself. That way she'd get back to Gabe all the sooner.

Jane jumped to her feet as Lucy burst through the shop door. "Lucy—?" she began.

Lucy waved an imperious hand to shut Jane up. "Ambulance," she said curtly into her phone. "At the Bliss Nursery. There's been an accident with a falling tree branch. Gabriel Bliss is injured and unconscious." The despatcher asked various things about Gabe's condition. "I can't tell you any of that. I'm not with him. There's no phone signal where he is. But when I left him, he was breathing and his pulse was easy to find, though a bit unsteady. I haven't moved him in case there's spinal damage."

Jane, listening wide-eyed, swallowed a gasp. Muffin, sensing something bad was happening, gave an anxious yelp.

"As soon as the ambulance is on its way," Lucy went on, "I'll go back to him. Send the ambulance to the nursery shop. Jane Giddens here will direct it to where he is in the arboretum." She glanced across at Jane who was nodding eagerly. "Thank you," Lucy said to the despatcher. "Please come quickly."

"Did you get all that, Jane?" Lucy asked, tucking her phone into the pocket of her filthy trousers.

"Yes." Jane looked truly worried. And she wasn't asking loads of questions, which was unusual for Jane.

Lucy explained precisely where Gabe was in the arboretum so that Jane could direct the ambulance. "I've left him with my coat over him," she finished. "It'll keep the rain off, but it's not very warm."

"Hang on one minute. I'll get something from upstairs." Jane seemed to have recovered from the initial shock and was sounding more like her normal, sensible self. She ran for the stairs to the flat above the shop. In barely a minute, she was back, carrying a bundled duvet. "I stole this from Gabe's bed. I didn't bother with pillows. You won't want to move his head."

"Bless you." Lucy grabbed the bundle and ran for the door.

"I'll pack some things for Gabe while I'm waiting for the ambulance," Jane called after her. "They'll want to take him to the Queen Mary—"

Lucy didn't wait to hear the rest. She knew she could rely on Jane for the practical stuff. What mattered was to get back to Gabe. What if he regained consciousness and there was no one with him? What if he stopped breathing?

Back in the arboretum, Lucy parked as close to the cedar as she dared. It was still blowing hard and she didn't want to risk another branch flattening Maisie. She switched on her hazard lights to help the ambulance find her in the gathering gloom. Then she retrieved her multi-function torch from Maisie's boot and set it on the ground beside Gabe so that she could see better.

Gabe didn't seem to have moved. His eyes were still shut.

She knelt beside his prostrate body and leant close. Yes, he was still breathing. He didn't look great. But he didn't look worse, either.

She pulled off the raincoat, folded the duvet double and tucked it round him. Then she put her raincoat over the top. It didn't matter if Lucy got cold. Or wet. What mattered was to compensate for the wet and cold coming up from the ground he was lying on. It would help, too, if the rain would stop, but there was no sign of that.

She wanted to take him in her arms and hug him. But he mustn't be moved. At the same time, she wanted to thump him for his stupidity. She couldn't do that, either, so she raged at him, instead. "What on earth were you playing at, Gabe? You know cedars are dangerous in a storm. But you were only thinking about saving your precious tree, weren't you?" She swallowed tears of an emotion she didn't want to identify. "Oh, Gabe, you— One day, someone is going to tell you you're a prize idiot. Lovable, yes, but an idiot."

She fancied his lashes flickered a tiny bit just then. Oh help, had he heard what she'd just said? Please, no. She couldn't possibly face him if he knew how she felt about him. It would be humiliating.

Not daring to breathe, she fixed her eyes on his face.

His eyes didn't open. There was no sign at all that he was coming round. Lucy knew she shouldn't be relieved, but she was. Instantly, she felt guilty. So she tried to make amends by muttering practicalities about how soon help would be coming.

Finally, the ambulance arrived. With Jane. And a small holdall.

The paramedic was very complimentary. "Well done, miss. You haven't moved him."

"No, I didn't dare," Lucy croaked.

"Quite right. Leave it to us now." Within an amazingly short time, they had made their initial checks. Gabe, with his head and neck immobilised, was strapped to a stretcher and carried into the ambulance.

"Will you go with him, Jane?"

"Oh, I can't. I've left Muffin in my car at the shop."

"Don't worry. If you give me your keys, I'll go back and collect him. He can sit in Maisie while we're both inside. He'll be fine." When Jane nodded, Lucy reached for the holdall. "I'll take this. They won't want to be tripping over it in the ambulance." As the ambulance sped off, blue lights flashing, Lucy stuffed the bag, the duvet and her flashlight into the back of the Land Rover. She started to put her raincoat on, but soon gave up. She was too wet for a coat to be of any use at all. Especially a coat that was as sodden as the rest of her.

When Lucy caught up with Jane at the Queen Mary Hospital, she learned that Gabe had come round in the ambulance, but he'd been dazed and confused. Classic signs of concussion, the medics said. They were going to keep him in overnight while they did more tests. "They asked about his next of kin," Jane went on. "There must be someone, but I've no idea who. Do you know?"

Lucy shook her head. Gabe was an only child and his parents were dead.

"Well, it'll have to be us, then," Jane said. "You and me, lovey."

"Yes, you're right," Lucy agreed, much struck.

"Someone will have to look after him when they let him out. They won't want him to be alone in the upstairs flat at night."

"No. And he isn't going to be," Lucy said, with decision. "He can come back to the Manor House and we'll look after him there. After a concussion, he shouldn't be on his own."

Jane reached out a hand to pat Lucy on the shoulder and then changed it to a big, warm hug. "You are a smashing girl, Lucy Cairns. I'd have offered myself, but we don't have the room. Besides, I need to be at the shop, so I couldn't be at home looking after Gabe."

"Don't worry, Jane. It'll be fine." Well, it *would* be fine, provided Gabe didn't throw one of his tantrums and refuse to be the subject of Lucy's "charity".

Next day, once the doctors had finally established that there were no other injuries, Gabe was told he could leave, provided he was not left alone for at least forty-eight hours. Lucy grinned to herself when she heard that. Even Gabe would have trouble refusing her help this time.

And she had her tactics all worked out, in case he tried.

She persuaded her father to go with her to fetch Gabe from the hospital. She would let her dad do the talking while she retired to the furthest corner and tried to become invisible. In the face of Sir Drew's bluff kindness, even Gabe couldn't get on his high horse, could he?

It worked. "You'll come back to the Manor with us, of course." Sir Drew was clearly stating a fact, not issuing an invitation. "Lucy has made up the big front bedroom for you. And we'll be on hand for anything you need."

"But I couldn't—" Gabe started to shake his head and stopped abruptly. Lucy sympathised. Just a little. For Gabe, head-shaking probably was not a good idea. But she reminded herself that, if he weren't so stubborn, he wouldn't have tried doing anything so daft in the first place.

"Gabe, my boy, if you don't come to us, the hospital won't let you leave at all. There's no way they'll allow you to be in your flat on your own. Which you would be, at night. So you might as well give in now, eh? Besides, they're short of beds. It would be selfish of you to be blocking a bed here when you could be safe with us, don't you think?"

Game, set and match to Sir Drew.

Gabe smiled ruefully towards Lucy's corner and gave in.

Lucy, for her part, managed not to look too smug, though inwardly she was cheering.

The three of them were sharing a light supper in the Manor's cosy family kitchen. Gabe kept telling himself he shouldn't feel guilty about accepting his landlord's hospitality, but that argument wasn't working too well. Staying at the Manor might be the practical solution, but

Gabe still had a nagging feeling he'd betrayed his principles.

"Lucy thought you shouldn't eat anything too rich, Gabe." Sir Drew gestured to the simple fare she had set out. "The doctors said we mustn't overtax your system. And certainly no alcohol," he added with a sly grin, topping up his own wine glass. Sir Drew was kindness itself, but he did enjoy a joke.

Like Gabe, Lucy was drinking plain water. In solidarity with the invalid? Or maybe she was just wiped, after all the running around she had been doing for him. The woman was a life-saver. Possibly literally so. What would have happened to him if he'd lain undiscovered for hours in that storm? Especially as it was his own stupid fault for trying to save part of a tree that couldn't be saved.

As soon as their meal was finished, Sir Drew took Gabe upstairs and showed him to his bedroom. It was, as promised, at the front of the house, overlooking the drive and the lawn. It was huge, bigger than the whole of Gabe's little flat.

And it was decidedly opulent.

"I hope you'll be comfortable here, Gabe. Lucy has put your shaving things and so on in the bathroom, there—" he gestured towards a half-open door that obviously led to the ensuite bathroom "—and your clothes are hanging in the wardrobe. You can tell how worried she was about you. Look, she's even hung your pyjamas on the radiator so you won't be cold when you get ready for bed."

Lucy's thoughtfulness was rather more than Gabe could cope with right at that moment. It had been unsettling enough to see himself pictured as Lucy's husband in the museum, but at least, in the image, the two of them had been standing decorously side by side. This was so much more intimate.

Tactful as ever, she'd allowed her father to do the honours in the bedroom, but Gabe could *feel* her presence. His mind was suddenly swirling with disturbing images: Lucy's hands setting out his wash kit in the bathroom; Lucy caressing his clothes onto hangers and over a radiator. All for his comfort. As a loving wife might do. He gulped. If Lucy had been here in the bedroom with him, he might well have done something he'd regret.

"The heating stays on all night. Not at full pelt, of course, but enough to ensure these huge rooms don't get too draughty. I wanted to install full double glazing, but the planners wouldn't allow it. Listed building, you know?"

Gabe didn't know, but he agreed anyway. Right now, he was too confused and weary for this kind of conversation. He wanted nothing more than his bed, and a soft pillow under his aching head.

"Sorry, I'm rambling on. I'll leave you to get undressed. I'm sure you're ready for your bed."

Gabe grunted assent.

Sir Drew made for the door. "There's a phone by the bed. If you need anything, dial 11 for Lucy and 22 for me. We'll be happy to come and help."

"But I couldn't—"

"Yes, you could. I insist. You've had a nasty shock, and a nasty injury. You're here with us until you're fully recovered. And, as your friends, Gabe, we want to help. Please do let us. We'll be really hurt if you don't."

There was nothing Gabe could possibly say in response. So, when Sir Drew mentioned the phone again, Gabe promised he'd call them if he felt at all unwell in the night. Apparently satisfied, Sir Drew went back downstairs.

*Please don't let me have to call for help. I couldn't bear to be any more beholden to the Cairns. Especially not to Lucy.*

The ensuite bathroom was warm and luxurious. It was almost as big as the bedroom, with his-and-hers handbasins, mirrors everywhere, and the thickest, softest, whitest towels Gabe had ever used. Tomorrow, perhaps, he'd have a long soak in the tub, but for now, he didn't have the energy. He managed to clean his teeth and splash his face with water. That was his lot. He was utterly knackered.

Five minutes later, he was climbing into the huge double bed. He discovered there was even a hot water bottle in it.

Lucy again. Warm pyjamas and a warm bed. She had a very warm heart. And her pillows were deliciously soft. He turned on his side, sinking deeper into the sweet-smelling luxury. It wasn't his thing, of course—he was only a menial—but just this once, he'd allow himself to be indulged. He *had* been concussed so he was allowed a bit of pampering, wasn't he?

He closed his eyes, snuggled down even further and let his mind drift…

# Chapter Six

WHEN GABE WOKE UP, he felt like a new man. Lighter. Freed. As if a great weight had been lifted off him. As if he were floating. He lay still in the huge bed, eyes closed, relishing the feelings of release and luxuriating in the softness enfolding him.

But he'd had a concussion. He needed to check…

Gingerly, he turned his head on the pillow. No dizziness. Good. But—

*Good grief! What on earth…?*

He touched a hand to his cheek. He wasn't mistaken. Someone had stuck long bushy sideburns on him while he was out for the count. That was beyond a joke, however funny the culprit thought it was. And Gabe certainly wasn't going to put up with it. He seized some of the offending cheek hair between his finger and thumb and tugged hard to free the glue.

*Ouch!* It really hurt. These sideburns weren't stuck on. They were growing. They were his.

*What the hell…?*

He heard the bedroom door open. He turned his head—carefully—and saw that his visitor was a portly, bewhiskered man dressed in the formal black that a servant would have worn in a previous century. Victorian, maybe? The man was carrying a tray. "Good morning, sir. I've brought your breakfast, as you ordered." He crossed the room to deposit his tray on a side table. He began to draw the heavy curtains back. It was a bright sunny morning. Much too bright for Gabe's reeling senses.

What on earth was going on? Was Gabe having a nightmare? Or hallucinating? He'd had a blow to the head, so anything was possible.

But Gabe's sideburns couldn't be a hallucination, could they? He put his hand to his other cheek. Yes, matching whiskers there. He tried pulling again, more gently this time. The second set wasn't stuck on, either. They were the real deal.

*At least I don't have a beard.* The thought popped into his mind, from nowhere. And it was funny. Sort of. He'd always hated beards. The full bushy Charles Darwin look came latish in Victoria's reign, he remembered. So this hallucination must be earlier. When the fashion was only for side-whiskers.

*About the time of that daguerreotype in the museum. Is* that *it? Is that what's causing this weird vision? Maybe I'm recreating the image in which I was lord of the manor. And married to dear, sweet Lucy.*

That might be worth a blow on the head.

Another random thought struck him. He found himself wondering why his hallucination hadn't provided the luscious Lucy in bed beside him. Had she already gone down to breakfast, perhaps? Surreptitiously, he ran his hand over the pillow alongside him. No dent where her head might have lain, sadly. But maybe she'd smoothed her pillow? While the servant was still fussing with the curtains, Gabe quickly sniffed the linen. And his heart sank. If she'd slept beside him, there would have been some trace of her sweet scent, wouldn't there? But there was nothing at all. Unless Victorian toffs had separate bedrooms? He hadn't a clue whether they did or not, but it was the only plausible explanation he could think of, right now.

The servant came across to help Gabe sit up, placing extra pillows—including the ones that should have been Lucy's—behind his back. Then he fetched the tray.

Gabe needed to question this man about his wife. But how? He couldn't very well ask why his wife wasn't in bed with him. With his brain in turmoil, there was no sensible question he *could* ask.

So he waved the breakfast tray away and slid back down into the bed. "Argh. I find I am unwell this morning," he lied. "Not at all myself. Dizzy. With a searing headache. Draw those curtains against the light, if you please."

The servant silently removed the tray and went to do as he was bid.

"My wife...?" Gabe said quietly, but with a distinct question in his voice.

The servant stopped dead in the act of closing the curtains. Then, after a second, he completed his task. "You are clearly not yourself, sir, as you say. I will ask Cook to prepare a tisane for you."

Gabe wasn't having any of their Victorian potions. They'd probably poison him. What he wanted was Lucy. Now. "Ask my wife to join me here, if you please," he ordered.

The servant was rigid, staring at the floor. "Sir, er..."

He swallowed hard. "Sir, you are not married."

Would the manservant assume Gabe had been raving, describing some kind of alcohol-fuelled vision? Gabe hoped so. What other explanation could the man come up with, anyway? Nothing else even began to make sense. Still, to cement the idea in the servant's mind, Gabe would keep to his room for the rest of the day and exhibit all the signs of a monumental hangover. It was the best he could do.

He'd made a complete pig's ear of things by assuming that he'd somehow been transposed to the world of the daguerreotype, complete with wife. What an idiotic notion that was.

He had to be having some kind of dream, or hallucination. And, sadly, Lucy was not part of the deal. It was really mean of his imagination to have left her out, but he was clearly to have no choice in the matter. Possibly it was better if his baser desires did not figure in this episode, in any case. He would wait until the dream—or nightmare, or whatever it was—wore off. It was bound to fade, eventually, wasn't it? And then he'd be back in Lucy's best spare bedroom, in the twenty-first century. With his baser instincts under the tightest possible control. And without uppity servants looking down their noses at him.

In the course of the day, the same servant appeared several times, sometimes with a footman in tow. Gabe discovered that the servant with the breakfast tray was, in fact, the butler rather than a mere valet. He didn't discover the man's name, unfortunately. But he told himself that, if he listened carefully to the other servants, he should soon be able to find out what it was.

The footman was called Charles. Gabe suspected that

the man's name might be something else altogether—
possibly something much more working-class.
Nineteenth-century employers often insisted on retaining
the same names for new servants, because it was too
much trouble to learn what their given names were.
Footmen were, in that sense, interchangeable. Was
nineteenth-century Gabe, the master, such an unfeeling
man? He hoped not, but a nagging doubt remained. It felt
very unsettling to think that he might have anything at all
in common with such an employer. He, of all people,
knew what it felt like to be treated like a non-person. But
maybe he was overreacting? Maybe the footman actually
was called Charles? He resolved to find out. And, if
necessary, to restore the footman's real name.

By the middle of the afternoon, Gabe was beginning
to feel hungry. He needed to eat something. What should
a man with a foul hangover ask for? No, wrong. What
would a *Victorian* man with a foul hangover ask for? A
modern man might go for the comfort of toast and tea
but, for all Gabe knew, a Victorian might demand sirloin
of beef and port wine.

He scanned the walls for a bell. The servants had
been in and out so often, Gabe hadn't needed to summon
anyone until now. But there should be a bell-push
somewhere.

He couldn't see one.

No, of course not. Electric bells came later. Any bells
in this house would have to be mechanical. Ah, yes,
there it was. The tasselled silk rope hanging by the side
of the bed was not simply another piece of
ornamentation in this over-decorated room, he realised;
it was actually a bell pull. He reached out and tugged.

The butler appeared unexpectedly quickly. "You
rang, sir?" His voice was very soft. Was be pandering to

the master's supposedly aching head? Had he been lurking outside the bedroom door?

Gabe ran the back of his hand across his forehead and sighed affectedly. "I did. I will admit to feeling remarkably under the weather today. I assume it must have been something I ate," he lied smoothly. No master would admit to being unable to hold his liquor, surely? Even to the butler who had probably witnessed the downing of every last glass.

The butler, straight-faced, said only, "Indeed, sir," in the sort of Jeeves voice that neither agreed nor disagreed.

"However, I am somewhat improved now and I should like something to eat. Be so good as to have a tray sent up to me here. I do not plan to leave this room today."

"As you wish, sir. I will arrange that immediately. Would you prefer to drink claret or burgundy, sir?"

Good grief! The Victorians obviously believed in the hair of the dog. But at least the man wasn't suggesting port. Gabe managed not to laugh. "On this occasion, I find I do not care. Send up whatever you think appropriate."

The butler looked startled but all he said was, "Yes, sir. Charles will bring up the tray the moment it is ready. Is there anything else you would like?"

"No." Gabe waved a dismissive hand. "That will be all."

About half an hour later, Charles appeared, with a loaded tray. And a full bottle of burgundy.

Gabe sat up in bed and allowed the footman to place the tray across his lap. "Burgundy?" he said, with a question in his voice.

"Well, sir, Mr Weir said as burgundy wine was more suitable for this. Sir."

*Ah. My butler's name is Weir.*

"And what do you think, Charles?" Gabe asked mischievously.

"Me, sir? I...I don't know nothing about wines. Not yet, I don't."

"But you are keen to learn?"

"Oh, yes, sir."

"Excellent. Hard work will always be rewarded in my house. Remind me, Charles. Is that your given name?"

The footman started and swallowed at the master's strange question. "Well, me mam calls me 'Charlie', but I suppose it's the same, really."

"Indeed it is. And how long have you been in my employ, Charles?"

"Five months, come Saturday, sir," the footman said proudly. "I do hope to have given satisfaction," he added, sounding rather less confident.

"Does Mr Weir think you give satisfaction, Charles?"

The footman busied himself with straightening the bedclothes so that his expression was hidden. "I couldn't say, sir, I'm sure. I have done my best to learn my duties, sir. I hope I've given no cause for complaint."

It sounded as though the butler was a typical martinet. All kicks and no ha'pence, as they used to say? Did he ever give a word of praise to his underlings?

"I am more than satisfied, Charles," Gabe said firmly. "You need have no worries on that score." The footman's shoulders visibly relaxed. So he had been worried.

If Gabe was going to stay in this dream for much longer, he would make it his business to find out whether his house was well run and whether the staff were fairly treated and properly paid. If the staff were fulfilling their duties, he would thank them, personally. That would probably be a first! Revolutionary, even.

Gabe lifted the covers from his food. Lamb cutlets, a fluffy omelette dotted with herbs, and a plate of bread and butter on the side. Pretty robust fare for a man with a hangover, but just at the moment, Gabe felt he could do justice to every last morsel. "Thank you, Charles. This will do me very well. You may pour me a glass of wine. Leave the bottle. I will serve myself if I want more."

When he woke up next morning, Gabe's first move was to check for side-whiskers. Unfortunately for him, they were still there, still growing, still driving him nuts. So his crazy dream hadn't worn off yet.

He sighed and reached for the bell pull. No more excuses. Today he would be up and doing. Since he was here, he wanted to find out more about his estate and the people who worked for him. And if he could manage an old-fashioned straight razor, he might even shave off his wretched side-whiskers.

The razor, he discovered, was beyond him. In the end, he gave up and sent for Charles to shave him. So the whiskers had to stay. Gabe excused his own failings by saying that his hands were still a bit shaky. Convincing enough, from someone who was supposed to have been on an almighty bender. But it wasn't an excuse he could rely on for long. Eventually, he would have to teach himself how to shave with a cut-throat.

Or maybe he should start an early fashion for a full beard?

That made Gabe laugh aloud. At himself. Was he not the man who regularly said that beards were the devil's work? It seemed he was as ready to compromise his principles as those twenty-first century politicians he so despised.

\* \* \*

After a day of riding round the Home Farm and visiting some of his nearest tenants, Gabe was really sore. He could ride well enough, of course—as a country boy, he'd been put on a horse almost as soon as he could walk—but his twenty-first century body hadn't hauled itself into the saddle for quite a few years. So it was objecting to the exercise. In spades. And now he'd made the additional mistake of sinking into the chair in his study. He wasn't sure he could get out of it again.

Not that he dare allow that to show here in his strange vision. For a Victorian landowner, riding or driving a horse would be as natural as walking. For Gabe, who had never learned to drive any kind of horse-drawn vehicle apart from a trundling farm cart, it had had to be the saddle. And the saddle-sores.

He'd been relatively satisfied with what he'd found on his land, though. To his modern eye, the tenant farms seemed well run and the cottages where the families lived, while very modest, were structurally sound and clean. He had seen no leaking roofs or crumbling walls. He had seen lots of neat, productive vegetable gardens, well-tended pastures and healthy livestock. His tenants had welcomed him into their homes, even offering jugs of ale to slake his thirst. It had been good ale, too. They had greeted him with respect, but also with a degree of warmth, even though there was a clear distance between them. He could do nothing about that; his single attempt to be more friendly had been met with frosty politeness. He'd learned his lesson from that and had not made the same mistake during the rest of his tour.

Gabe was less sure about his own household. A single day was not long enough to be certain, but he was very uneasy about the way some of the indoor servants scuttled about, apparently not daring to look him in the

71

eye. Were they terrified of a master who raved about a non-existent wife? They never spoke, unless spoken to. Not even "Good morning, sir." Maybe Victorian households were expected to be silent, and barely even seen? Gabe vaguely remembered something from his history reading, something about servants turning to face the wall if they met their betters on the staircase. Not a comfortable explanation, but preferable to fear of a mad master.

The only member of staff who ventured to speak to Gabe was Weir, the butler. Gabe found he could not warm to the man, although he could not put his finger on why. Weir seemed to run an efficient household. Did he rule through fear? Gabe resolved to find out more. A butler would have the power to ruin any servant's career, even though it was nominally the master or mistress who hired and fired.

Gabe leafed quickly through the correspondence on his desk. A few invitations, some business matters, but nothing urgent. He pushed them aside and glanced at the little clock above the fireplace. He had barely half an hour. And it was his own fault. Weir had reminded him, as he was mounting his horse, that dinner would be served in the late afternoon, as usual, unless Gabe chose to put it back. Gabe had waved the suggestion aside and ridden off. But now what he wanted was a long soak in a hot bath, to ease his aching muscles. He was master here, wasn't he? So he could change his mind, even if it disrupted his household's country hours.

He almost laughed at his own attitude. Wasn't he the man who objected to employers who ordered their servants about like slaves? And wasn't he doing precisely that? Perhaps he should simply go upstairs and change for dinner, so as not to disrupt the house's routine.

He made to get up and do so. But his muscles ached so much he could barely move. No. It would have to be disruption. For the sake of the master's maltreated body.

Gabe rang the bell.

Weir appeared very promptly, smiling in the obsequious way that so irked Gabe. Was it because of that smile that he distrusted the man? Or was he sensing something more?

"I should like a hot bath before dinner, Weir. I take it you can arrange that?"

"*Before* dinner, sir?" The butler glanced at the clock. "Would you not perhaps rather—"

"No, Weir. I am filthy and I stink of horse after a long day in the saddle." That was a good enough reason. No need to mention his aches and pains. "I want a bath before dinner. See to it, if you please."

The man was twisting his hands together. "I will see to it at once, sir." He made no move to leave the study.

Gabe raised an eyebrow at him.

"I beg your pardon, sir, but there is a minor matter I must bring to your attention."

"Urgent, is it?" Gabe demanded sarkily.

"I think so, sir."

Gabe sat back in his chair. "Very well. I am listening."

"I...I discovered a maid in a compromising position with one of the footmen earlier, while you were out."

"Indeed?" What on earth did "a compromising position" mean? A kiss? Or full-blown sex? Gabe needed to know more. "Where, precisely, did you find them?"

The butler looked startled by the question. "On...on the back stairs, sir."

So just a quick fumble? Was it so very dreadful if a pair of servants risked a moment of mutual warmth?

"And what are you proposing to do about it, Weir?"

"The woman should leave at once, sir. Without a character. I cannot be— No butler can be expected to run a respectable household with a woman of loose morals in it. I presume I have your permission to dismiss her?"

"And the footman in the case?" Gabe asked quietly.

"He is a good man, sir, but too easily led astray by a wanton. I will warn him about his conduct, of course, and I am sure he will not err again."

Gabe didn't like this. Not one bit. Who was this pair anyway? The situation needed a lot more investigation. It was all too pat. If two members of his staff had broken the rules, why should the woman be thrown into the gutter and the man emerge unscathed? It might be the Victorian way, but it was not Gabe's way.

"I will see the woman and question her for myself."

The butler's eyes widened and he took an involuntary step backwards. "I…I would not dream of asking you to take the trouble, sir. Her dismissal is purely a formality, after all. Any well-regulated household would do the same. Indeed, I am sure it is what she expects. And, of course, it is part of my duties to take care of such mundane matters for you. May I be excused now? I need to give the orders for your bath."

Gabe narrowed his eyes and leaned forward. "I should perhaps remind you, Weir, that this is *my* household and I pay the staff. Including you. I will see the woman myself. Now. What is her name?"

"Er…Cairns."

Gabe rocked back in his seat. For several seconds, he couldn't speak. Or breathe. It was as if Weir had thumped him in the gut. He found himself staring impotently at the man. And hating him.

His better self came to his rescue. *You've gone this*

74

*far, Gabe. You can't give in now. It's a matter of principle. And justice.*

"Cairns," Gabe repeated hoarsely. "Very well. I will see her now. Bring her in, if you please. Does she have a name besides Cairns? A Christian name?"

"I...I am not sure, sir. I think it may be Lucy."

Gabe was truly winded this time. And his head was reeling. So the woman in the daguerreotype was not Gabe's wife after all, but a servant? How on earth did that make sense?

Gabe's memory of the daguerreotype seemed to wobble from positive to negative, as unstable as a mirage. Had he really seen himself with Lucy? And what was happening in this weird, other-worldly nightmare?

It seemed he was about to confront Lucy Cairns. Not Lucy Cairns, Gabe's almost-boss, but Lucy Cairns the lowly servant, whose future as a respectable member of below-stairs society depended totally on Gabriel Bliss.

# Chapter Seven

"HERE IS CAIRNS, SIR." Weir's tone was funereal.

The offending maid, Lucy—for it was most definitely Lucy, in spite of the plain black gown and the scraped-back fair hair—shot a glance of utter contempt at the butler and marched into the room. She stopped in front of Gabe's desk and looked down at him. There was a glint of battle in her eyes, too.

Before Gabe could open his mouth, she said, in the businesslike voice that he recognised, "I am not one of your maids, sir, though you may be unaware of it. I am the assistant housekeeper. Mrs Cairns."

Ah. That explained the dark gown and the absence of an apron. And housekeepers were always dignified by being called "Mrs", even when they were unmarried. So what had Weir been playing at, suggesting Lucy was merely a maid, to be addressed by her surname? Gabe glanced across to the door where the butler stood. He was looking increasingly shifty. Guilty, even.

Right. Gabe was going to get to the bottom of this.

"Thank you, Weir. You may leave us."

"But sir—"

"I will interview Mrs Cairns alone. You have other duties to see to. Including—may I remind you?—my bath."

"Oh. Yes, sir." Weir gave a stiff little bow from the neck and backed out.

Once the door was safely closed, Gabe smiled up at Lucy. He wanted her confidence. He didn't want her frightened. Though, to be honest, she didn't look in the least afraid, more like an Amazon preparing herself for war. He reminded himself that she did not really know him, except as the master of the house, and she had no reason to trust him. She looked like his Lucy, but she was someone else entirely.

"Please sit down." He gestured to the chair on the other side of his desk.

"No, thank you, sir. I would rather stand."

Gabe managed not to smile. Lucy's doppelgänger knew how to keep the advantage. But he would not have her looking down on him, even in a situation like this, where he was the boss and she the underling. So he forced his creaking muscles out of the chair and made his way across to the fire. He leaned against the mantelpiece, trying to appear nonchalant. Given the way her gaze narrowed, he wasn't sure he was succeeding. "Weir has told me why he wishes to dismiss you. Now I would like to hear your side of the story." He was being strictly neutral. "The truth, if you please," he added firmly.

Lucy's eyebrows rose a fraction. Had she been expecting a dressing-down? Probably. He watched her take a couple of deep breaths. Her bosom rose and fell distractingly. Gabe forced himself to focus on her face, instead. He said nothing. He simply waited.

After a moment she made up her mind. "It will not be long in the telling, sir," she said crisply. "I was accosted on the back stairs. My assailant forced me against the wall. He kissed me and he put his hands under my skirts. I succeeded in fighting him off. That is all."

"You were not a willing participant?"

Lucy shuddered. "I was not," she spat.

"And Weir saved you from this assault? He saw it?"

Lucy sagged for a second. Then she straightened her shoulders again and drew herself up. "Mr Weir did not prevent the assault. Mr Weir was the assailant."

Gabe was so shocked he was lost for words. He stared at her. In the back of his mind, a little voice muttered that it explained a great deal. No wonder the butler was in such a hurry to dismiss Lucy without a hearing.

Eventually, she broke the silence by saying, "I see that you do not believe me. I expected nothing else. I have no witnesses, after all. But I hope you will not deny me a reference, at least?" When Gabe still failed to respond, she said, with exaggerated politeness, "Then if you will kindly excuse me, sir—" she even dropped a little curtsey "—I must go and pack my box. Might I ask for the use of the gig to take me to town? It is a long way and it will soon be dark."

"You will be going nowhere in my gig," Gabe exclaimed.

Lucy's expression hardened. She lifted her chin. "Very well, sir. I will walk."

"You will do no such thing. You are going nowhere." He swallowed. "I beg your pardon. That sounded much too abrupt. I have let my anger show but it is not directed at you, I assure you. Will you not sit down?" He gestured to the chair again. "Please?"

Lucy looked a little bewildered but, after a second or two, she sank into the chair.

In spite of his aches, Gabe crossed to the side table where he poured two glasses of Madeira. He handed the smaller one to Lucy. "Here. Drink this. You have had a truly shocking experience and I am heartily sorry that it should have happened in a house of mine."

Still looking stunned, she took the glass from him and sipped. Then she sipped again, with more confidence. Was she beginning to see that Gabe was on her side? And prepared to go into battle on her behalf?

"I am not a fool, Mrs Cairns." This new Lucy needed protection. And he was the one to provide it. If she would only trust him. He smiled down at her. "Or Lucy, if I may?"

She neither nodded nor shook her head. She said nothing. In her position, she probably felt she could not. But her rigid posture told Gabe he had gone much too far. Was he making her think that he was another lecher, like Weir?

"Your pardon, again. I should not have presumed so. 'Mrs Cairns' it shall be. As I said, Mrs Cairns, I am not a fool. I recognise the truth when I hear it. And I know I have heard it from you."

She jerked her head up to stare at him. In her hand, the crystal glass shook; a drop of Madeira spilled onto her black skirt. She didn't seem to notice. "You believe me?" She sounded astonished.

"I do. Now, finish your Madeira, Mrs Cairns, and tell me the truth about this household of mine. There are clearly things that I need to know."

It was as bad as Gabe had feared. Weir pretended to be a righteous, god-fearing man but he was actually a household tyrant. Especially to the younger females. The housekeeper, Mrs Neville, old and infirm and half-blind, did nothing to protect the women, perhaps because she no longer noticed what was going on. Weir was crafty about concealing his assignations with the maids, Lucy said, so it would be fair to give Mrs Neville the benefit of the doubt over that. The old housekeeper was about to retire, after all. That was why Weir had given Lucy temporary (and unpaid) promotion from maid to assistant housekeeper. She was to learn Mrs Neville's duties and then to take over the role. The transition was to be so seamless that the master would notice nothing until Lucy was presented to him as Mrs Neville's successor. A *fait accompli*.

And one that Lucy believed the butler was planning to exploit.

Gabe could well imagine what Weir was planning to demand by way of payment.

"I've managed to avoid his, um, his advances, so far. Most of the time," Lucy went on. "Most of his attention is devoted to—" She stopped, clearly embarrassed at having to talk in detail about Weir's lechery. "He, er, he is particularly friendly with one of the maids, who does not object. But he has a roving eye and I fear he is seeking another conquest. He enjoys the chase so much, you see. Especially when his prey is unwilling." She swallowed hard. "Perhaps because I have resisted him so far, he seems to have fixed on me."

Gabe fetched the decanter and poured more Madeira for her. "Please take your time, Mrs Cairns. But tell me the rest."

"I need this post, sir. And this promotion. I have an aged father to support, you see. But I knew it was going to be difficult once Mrs Neville finally retired. Cook and

I and Mr Weir would be in the housekeeper's room after meals and…and Cook tends to doze off when she's taken a glass of wine. Mr Weir, I am sorry to report, is very generous with your wine, so Cook usually ends up sound asleep in her chair."

Gabe didn't give a toss about the wine. But he cared very much about Lucy being unable to escape from Weir's groping hands.

"The man is a disgrace. He shall leave my house today!"

"Sir, you have no proof."

"I have you, Mrs Cairns."

She managed a half-hearted smile, but she was shaking her head. "No one else will take the word of a jumped-up maid against a butler with a spotless reputation. It is the way of the world. My world, at least," she added sadly. "I would never be able to find another post if you were to dismiss Mr Weir on my account."

But Lucy wouldn't need to find another post. Gabe would fire Weir and Lucy would stay on in his household, as housekeeper. It was simple, surely?

His expression must have betrayed his thoughts. She shook her head at him once more. "There would be gossip, sir. Mr Weir is known all round the county as a fine, upstanding butler, a man with decades of unblemished service. People would not believe that he was taking advantage of the women of the household." She fixed her gaze on her skirts and her voice dropped to a hesitant whisper. "But they would believe it of *you*. It is well known that some masters do, er, take advantage of innocent servants. The gossips would say you were pandering to the whims of a servant girl for reasons of your own. Dishonourable ones."

Oh. Unfortunately, that sounded all too plausible. "So what would you have me do?" Gabe asked.

She looked up, startled. "Why, nothing, sir. It is not my place to give instructions to you."

Gabe growled and began to pace, his muscles easing gradually. If he couldn't fire Weir, he had to save Lucy.

And—*eureka!*—he had the beginnings of a plan.

"Where does your father live, Mrs Cairns?"

She named a small village on the far side of the town, several miles away.

"Excellent. Now go and pack your box and be ready to leave in half an hour."

She put a hand to her throat. She had gone pale. "You are dismissing me, sir?"

"No, Mrs Cairns, I am sending you on holiday. Paid, of course. But to somewhere safe. And—"

The study door opened. It was Weir.

Lucy's reaction was lightning-fast. She hadn't time to rise from her chair but she hid the Madeira glass in her skirts and bowed her head. She looked as if she had just received a jail sentence.

"Your bath is prepared in your bedchamber, sir." Weir glanced at Lucy and then away again. His expression was inscrutable.

"Good. I will be up in a moment. In the meantime, send a message to the stables for my gig and a dependable groom. Mrs Cairns and her belongings are to be conveyed to her father's house. She will be leaving us tonight."

"For good?" Weir asked, wide-eyed.

"Did you expect anything less?" Gabe countered sharply, avoiding a direct lie.

Weir spluttered something that might have been an apology.

"But we are wasting time. If you do not make haste with arranging the transport, it will be dark before she can set out and she will have to remain another night. I am sure you would prefer to avoid that."

Weir nodded. "It shall be done at once, sir." He puffed out his chest and bustled off.

Gabe turned back to Lucy. Her head was still bowed. "Mrs Cairns. Do not be afraid. I am going to deal with this matter. And I will ride over to see you, as soon as I can, to tell you what is happening. Please trust me on this. You will soon be back in your proper place here, I promise you. Without Weir to threaten you."

She rose, but did not return her empty glass to the table. "You will not wish Mr Weir to notice that two glasses have been used, sir. I will wash this one and return it to its place before I leave."

Gabe gave a snort of laughter. "You are clearly a born conspirator." He lifted her free hand to his lips and dropped a kiss on it. "I look forward to working with you, Mrs Cairns."

She blushed a deep, and very becoming, red. Then she dropped another curtsey and walked gracefully out of the room, closing the door very quietly at her back.

Days passed. Very, very slowly. And nothing changed, except that Gabe learned the detailed routine of his household and visited more of his tenants. His body adjusted to being in the saddle again; he no longer had to soak away a multitude of aches and pains at the end of each day.

Soon he might even try driving the gig, though he would need to ensure there was a steady horse between the shafts. Then it shouldn't be too different from a farm cart, should it?

It was a week since Lucy had left. Gabe missed her, far more than he'd imagined possible. Why should that be? He barely knew her, after all.

No, that wasn't true. He had only been with Lucy Cairns, assistant housekeeper, for a very short while, but he felt he knew her inside out. They had been friends as children—in the modern day, at least—and he had grown up liking and admiring her.

Loving her, even.

And that was the problem. He could admit it now. He loved Lucy Cairns. But he was a Victorian landowner, a toff; she, though clearly educated and well-mannered, was a member of the lower classes. The two were not supposed to meet, except as master and menial.

Hadn't he been telling Lucy that for months—years—in the modern day?

It was a bit of a shocker to have the tables turned on him like this. Could modern-day Lucy have been feeling as exasperated as Gabe was feeling now? Did she feel hamstrung by his insistence on stupid conventions? Impatient with the "rules" of their world that were coming between them?

And longing for what might have been?

Except that there were no might-have-beens here in this Victorian life. Gabe had power and wealth. And he didn't give a tinker's cuss for what other people thought of him. If he wanted this Lucy, he could go and get her, couldn't he?

Well, yes and no. She might be just as stubborn and pig-headed as modern-day Gabe. She might refuse to have anything to do with a man who had been her employer—and still was, in fact. Which reminded him…

"Why didn't I think of that before?" he said aloud. He would ride out to see her. Today. He had the perfect excuse. And perhaps when he did see her, he would be able to judge whether there was a chance for him.

For the two of them. Together.

# Chapter Eight

GABE SAID NOTHING TO Weir about visiting Lucy. He was riding to town, he said. He would probably have luncheon there and he might not return until late. The staff should not be surprised if dinner had to be put back. Again.

In the town, Gabe made a quick foray to a haberdasher's and ordered a dozen silk handkerchieves, for delivery to the Manor. That should be enough to allay any suspicions Weir might have. Some gentleman did spend hours selecting their linen, so why not Gabe also?

He avoided enquiring at the local inns—too many watching eyes and gossiping tongues—but managed to find a stray urchin who was only too pleased to put a fine gentleman on the road to Lucy's village in return for a penny. The boy was over the moon to find his reward was not a penny, but a silver sixpence.

Lucy's village was small but fairly prosperous and he found her cottage easily enough, next to the old Saxon church and not far from the local inn. Gabe rode into the inn yard and found an old man to look after his horse. "Give him a good rub down, will you? I may be some time."

The man tugged his forelock and promised that the horse would be well tended. He grinned toothily when Gabe produced some silver coins to seal the deal. "Thank 'ee, sir. Thank 'ee." The coins disappeared somewhere inside the man's moleskin waistcoat even before Gabe had turned back to the road.

Gabe had assumed that, since Lucy's aged father normally lived on his own, the cottage would show signs of neglect, lacking a woman's care. But he was wrong. The windows sparkled and the door looked to have been recently painted. Gabe decided, on the spot, that he would be unwise to make any kind of assumptions where Lucy was concerned.

The door opened only seconds after he let the knocker drop.

Lucy stood there. She was no longer wearing drab black. Her patterned blue cotton gown made her eyes look a deeper blue; and her fair hair was arranged becomingly. She looked delightful. But shocked to see him. She gasped out his name.

"Mrs Cairns." Gabe removed his hat, and bowed. "I have come, as I promised I would. I have something for you."

"You have news, sir?"

"Not exactly. I find I neglected to pay you your quarter's wages when you left. I have come to remedy that."

"Oh." She hesitated a moment, then stepped back to pull the door wide. "Will you not come inside, sir? Pa," she called into the dark interior of the cottage, "here is Mr Bliss, from the Manor."

Gabe followed Lucy inside. Once his eyes had become accustomed to the relative gloom, he saw that the room was neat and clean, with a pot bubbling at the edge of the fire. Its savoury smell made his mouth water and reminded him that he had had no food since an early breakfast. He hoped his stomach would not start to rumble.

An old man, presumably Lucy's father, was smoking a clay pipe in the inglenook but laid it aside and started to rise when Gabe approached. Lucy rushed to help him to his feet.

"Please do not disturb yourself on my account, Mr Cairns."

The old man straightened his back, though it was obvious that it pained him. "I may be slower than I once was, sir, but I can still stand to meet a guest," he said proudly, making a little bow. "Andrew Cairns, at your service, sir."

Gabe offered his hand. After a moment's hesitation, Cairns responded and the two men shook hands cordially. "I am delighted to make your acquaintance, Mr Cairns. I imagine you are pleased to have your daughter at home with you for a while?"

Cairns smiled and nodded.

"I am only sorry that I totally overlooked your daughter's wages when she left. Most remiss of me. So, by way of amends, I have brought her money with me today."

He dug into his pocket for the purse he had prepared and placed it in Lucy's hand. She nodded. Then she weighed it in her hand and frowned. To his surprise, she opened the purse and counted out the coins. "This is wrong, sir. It is more than I am owed."

"Mrs Cairns, you have been fulfilling the

housekeeper's duties in my household. I believe that the worker is worthy of his—or her—hire. What you have in your hand is a housekeeper's wage for the quarter. You are my housekeeper, since Mrs Neville is too infirm to perform the role. So you have earned this. All of it." He knew perfectly well that Weir had intended to pay Lucy only a maid's wage for the quarter, but Gabe would not tolerate such mean-minded dishonesty. Besides, she and her father probably needed the extra money. Winter was coming on and old Cairns did not look strong enough to cut wood or carry coals. If someone else was taking care of him, that someone else would have to be paid.

For a moment, Lucy seemed about to refuse, but then she sighed and nodded.

"You are a true gentleman, sir." Cairns nodded at Gabe. "Will you not be seated, here in the warm?" He waved a hand towards the inglenook and the old-fashioned rocking chair before the fire. "Lucy, girl, draw a jug of ale for our visitor."

Lucy smiled warmly at Gabe. "Certainly, I will, Pa. Unless Mr Bliss would prefer tea?"

Gabe returned her smile. He wasn't yet sure she trusted him. And he knew he needed to avoid alienating her father. "I am happy with either. Perhaps I might have whatever your father is having, Mrs Cairns?"

Old Cairns drew in a lungful of smoke and puffed it out. "Can't be doing with this new-fangled fashion for tea. Good old ale is what a man needs. That's what I say. A working man's drink for centuries."

"Then, if I may, Mrs Cairns, I will drink a jug of your ale."

"Of course. I will fetch it. And, since Pa and I were just about to sit down to our dinner, I hope you will join us? There's good mutton stew, with vegetables from our own garden. And bread from the bakery across the way."

"You are most kind. I should like that very much."
When Lucy left them to lay plates and cutlery on the
little table under the window, Gabe said, "Do you have
local help with the garden, sir? It must be hard work
turning the ground, especially in the winter."

Cairns held up one of his hands. All the joints were
swollen with arthritis and the fingers were crooked.
"Looks bad, don't it, sir? I may not be able to do fine
work any more, but it doesn't take much skill to pull
weeds and use a hoe. I'm not ready for my maker yet,
you know."

Gabe ignored that last bit. "What sort of fine work did
you do, sir?"

"I was—I still am—a master cabinet-maker, Mr Bliss.
That there chair you're sat on, I made. And that dresser
over there." He pointed to a beautiful piece of furniture
standing against the wall and shining with polish, even in
the half-light from the fire.

Gabe rose and crossed the room to admire it. The
workmanship was splendid. And now that he looked at
the rocking chair, its craftsmanship was exceptional, too.
"These are beautiful pieces, sir." He meant it. "It must
have been difficult to give up your craft."

"Didn't have no choice, sir. God chose to inflict these
pains on me—" he held up both hands this time, so that
Gabe could see the gnarled and twisted joints "—and I
have to bear them, as a Christian should."

In that moment, Gabe realised that Lucy's father was
not nearly as old as he looked. Pain and suffering had
aged him prematurely. He was probably no older than
Sir Drew, in Gabe's real world. But Sir Drew was hale
and hearty. And if he developed some horrid ailment,
like Mr Cairns, Sir Drew could afford to be treated by

the finest medics in the world. Here, Lucy's father probably had no medicine at all. No wonder he liked a drop of ale.

"I am sorry to see how you have had to suffer, Mr Cairns. I imagine it must be difficult for you to manage when your daughter is not here. Gardening is one thing, but preparing meals is rather more difficult, surely?"

"I can manage bread and cheese easily enough. And Mistress Brownlee brings me provisions and a hot meal most days." He nodded towards Lucy, now laying tumblers and a jug of water on the table. "Lucy and Mistress Brownlee are thick as thieves, I may tell you. I do believe that Mistress Brownlee reports to Lucy on everything I do."

Lucy laughed and came over to the fire. "That's not true, Pa, and you know it. Mistress Brownlee certainly tells me if you are unwell, or if you are not eating properly. But she's not spying on your every move, as you seem to suspect. She does only what I asked her to do. If I did not have someone to look in on you, I wouldn't be able to leave the village. And without my wages, where would we be?"

Cairns snorted, but then he relented a little and said, "Aye, well, there's some truth in that." He tried to ball his fists but failed. "If only these hands of mine would work as they should, there'd be no need for me to rely on you, my girl. You shouldn't be scrubbing someone else's floors and—"

"Housekeepers don't scrub floors, Pa," Lucy protested.

"—and suchlike," Cairns carried on regardless. "You should be settled with a home of your own. And children."

Gabe could see that poor Lucy was hugely

embarrassed by her father's words. There was nothing Gabe could say. It was much too soon to suggest that *he* might be the man to offer Lucy a home of her own.

"Pa, you are making our guest uncomfortable with such talk," Lucy said firmly. The old man glanced sideways at Gabe and grunted, but said nothing more. "Come," Lucy went on, gesturing towards the table, "let us enjoy the food the good Lord has given us."

It was a jolly meal. Both Lucy and Gabe were determined to keep the conversation light and amusing. After a while, Lucy's father joined in, too—possibly influenced by yet another jug of ale—and soon all three were laughing. The food was homely but so delicious that Gabe could not resist a second helping. "You are an excellent cook, Mrs Cairns." He smiled warmly at her. "Yet another quality that I was previously unaware of."

"Wait till you taste her apple pie." The old man was grinning.

"How did you know there was apple pie, Pa? I fetched it back from the baker's while you were out in the garden."

"My hands may not work, girl, but my nose still does." He grinned conspiratorially at Gabe. "Got some cream as well, have you, Lucy?"

Lucy laughed. "I have to tell you, sir, that my father insists on cream with apple pie. If there is no cream to be had, I daren't make the pie in the first place."

"I cannot think of a better dessert," Gabe said diplomatically. And he knew he'd been right as soon as she produced her pie. It had crisp, golden pastry and a tantalising aroma of caramelised fruit and cinnamon; she accompanied it with a blue pottery bowl piled high with thick yellow cream.

He had two helpings of pie, too. And then he sat back

in his chair with a sigh of contentment. "I think my horse will complain that I am now too heavy for him to carry me all the way back to the Manor."

Both Lucy and her father laughed at his feeble joke.

Meanwhile, Gabe was trying to work out what to do and say next. He wanted to call on Lucy again. Of course he did. But he must not presume. He must not call without an invitation. He must ask permission.

If only he could get Lucy alone to ask her.

Eventually, conversation petered out and Gabe rose to leave.

"Let me see you to the gate, sir," Lucy said demurely.

The moment they were outside on the path and her front door was shut, Gabe said, "May I call again, Mrs Cairns? Soon?"

"I do not think that would be wise, sir. If you are seen to be calling on a mere servant, there will be talk. You would not wish your reputation to be sullied by gossip."

Trust Lucy to worry about his reputation, rather than her own. "I am not concerned about my reputation, Mrs Cairns. However, I would not do anything that might sully yours. But if we do not meet alone—if your father is present, as he was today—surely there can be no gossip?" When she said nothing, Gabe shrugged and said, sadly, "But if you prefer that I leave you strictly alone, I will of course do so."

"Oh, but I don't—" She coloured. She had said too much. She stared at her feet and whispered, "My father and I would be most happy to see you here again, sir, if you wish to call on us."

Gabe smiled broadly but she was still staring at the ground so she could not see. He wanted to kiss her hand, but he did not dare to do anything so forward when the whole village might be watching. "Mrs Cairns, I accept

your invitation with the greatest pleasure," he said
gently. "And now, I must be on my way. I do not want to
be riding home in the dark, since that will give my poor
horse another reason to feel aggrieved."

She did look up and smile at that. When he bowed to
her, she responded with an elegant curtsey. Then she
returned to the house and closed the door, without
looking back at Gabe even once.


Gabe resolved not to visit Lucy the next day, much as he
wanted to. It was important to make his visits appear to
be a normal courtesy between neighbours, even though
the two households were not, strictly speaking,
neighbours. He also knew that employers rarely paid
calls on servants, but he did not care about that. Lucy
might well care, though. And he would do nothing to
upset her. He must be very discreet in everything he did.

Instead of a visit, Gabe would set himself to learning
to drive his gig. It would be delightful to drive out with
Lucy beside him, giving them a chance to talk freely in a
way that they could not do in Lucy's house with her
father listening to every word. But he dare not invite her
until he knew she would be safe with him. What if he
were to overturn them? He might do her real harm.

A one-horse gig shouldn't be any more difficult to
drive than a farm cart, should it? He shouldn't have
forgotten the skills. On the other hand, a heavy horse
tended to be slow and even-tempered. They were bred
for that. Gabe had no idea what kind of carriage horses
he had in his stable. Many wealthy gentlemen—and he
was sure he was one of those—filled their stables with
highly-strung horses that were difficult to manage. It was
the equivalent, he supposed, of driving a Ferrari in the
modern day. He'd never driven anything like that. And

he wasn't sure he'd be able to handle a temperamental horse, either.

Only one way to find out. He pulled the bell for his butler.

"Have a message sent to the stables, Weir. It's a fine day and I plan to go out driving. I will take the gig and the usual horse, if you please."

The butler's eyes widened. "The gig, sir? Would you not prefer your tilbury? Or your curricle? The gig is—"

"The gig is what I have chosen, Weir. I wish to judge for myself whether the vehicle, and the animal that normally pulls it, are still fit for use in my household. If they are not, then one or both will be changed. See that it is brought round without delay."

The butler gulped. "Of course, sir. At once."

Gabe smiled to himself as the butler closed the study door behind him. Since the gig was often used to fetch and carry servants and provisions, the usual horse was probably an easy creature to manage. With luck, Gabe would make it down his drive without any mishaps. It would be more than embarrassing if the watching servants began to wonder what had happened to the master's ability to control a single horse.

What's more, he now knew he had both a one-horse tilbury and a two-horse curricle. If the outing in the gig went well, he might be able to graduate to one of the others in the coming days. They would be more comfortable than the gig, especially for a lady passenger, but rather more difficult for Gabe to drive safely.

Time, and experiment, would decide.

The gig was a solid affair and the bay gelding in the shafts looked placid enough. Weir was watching from the open doorway as Gabe sprang up onto the wooden seat and took the reins with a confidence he didn't really feel. "I will probably be gone for some hours. Tell cook to prepare dinner for the normal hour but to be ready to delay it if I should be late."

Without waiting for Weir's reply, Gabe set the horse in motion and moved off sedately down the long drive to the gatehouse. By the time he reached his boundary, he realised that he had forgotten nothing. He might even be a better driver than he had dared to hope. Was that because he was not really twenty-first century Gabriel Bliss, but a nineteenth century version who had been driving since he was old enough to ride? Gabe hoped so, but he wasn't prepared to count on it. He decided to drive into town to check whether he could manage the traffic there. If it went well, he might even stop at the local inn for a bite to eat.

By the time he was driving down the town's main street towards the inn, he was smiling broadly. The traffic seemed to be no problem—although that might be simply because the horse was a canny animal—and he was feeling increasingly confident. Things were going well. Tomorrow, the tilbury?

*Never mind tomorrow, what about today? I could drive out to Lucy's now and ask her whether she would be prepared to accompany me on an outing. For an airing, nothing more. At a time of her choosing, of course. She couldn't be expected to come out with me today. But soon?*

It seemed a splendid idea. He would drive over and ask her.

This very afternoon.

He had already passed the side-road to Lucy's village so he had to turn the gig in the high street. That manoeuvre went remarkably well, too. Clearly nineteenth-century Gabe had had lots of practice.

Gabe was humming to himself as he retraced his path along the main street and turned off towards Lucy's village.

As Gabe drew up outside Lucy's house, he realised he had a problem. He had no groom and no one to hold the horse if he got down. He could drive the gig into the inn yard, of course, in hopes of finding the toothy old man, but what if Lucy was prepared to join him in the gig right now? He might miss a golden opportunity.

He was still trying to decide what to do when the door opened and Lucy herself came out. "Mr Bliss!" She hurried down the path to the gate but she did not open it. It remained a barrier between them. She was even resting her hands on the wood.

Gabe tipped his hat to her. "Good afternoon, Mrs Cairns. Forgive me, I may not get down to greet you as I have no groom to take the reins. I hope I find you well?"

Lucy nodded and smiled.

"And your father, also?"

"Yes, indeed. He has been in excellent spirits all day. Your visit yesterday cheered him a great deal."

"I am glad to hear it. I, um… It is such a fine day that I decided to go driving. And while I was enjoying the sunshine and the fresh air, it occurred to me that you might welcome a chance to go out for an airing. I imagine you have been cooped up in the house, or in the village, since you left the Manor. Might a change of scene be welcome?"

"Are you inviting me to go driving with you, sir?"

"Why, yes. Yes, I am." When he noticed the beginnings of a frown on her face, he added quickly, "At your convenience, of course, Mrs Cairns. I did not mean today, this moment. I would not so presume." That wasn't exactly true, but it might smooth over an invitation that probably sounded over-familiar.

It made no difference. Her frown deepened and she shook her head. "I am conscious of the honour, sir, but it would not do. A servant does not drive around alongside her master. Your neighbours would think very poorly of you if they saw us together. And even if they did not see us, they would soon hear of it. So, no. Thank you, but no."

He was making a complete pig's ear of this. He'd been hasty and selfish. Again. He grabbed for the first lifeline he could think of. "Perhaps your father would like to join us? There is room enough for three." It might do the trick. If they drove out as a threesome first time round, they might be able to be a twosome later.

Lucy smiled knowingly at that. Gabe had the distinct impression that she had seen through his desperate ruse. "I am afraid that the roads hereabouts are not well maintained, sir. Even in your fine vehicle, the jolting would be painful for my father. He suffers enough as it is. So, again, my answer must be no."

Gabe felt himself reddening as he realised that he had been thinking only of his own desires and giving no thought to Lucy's needs, or her father's. "Forgive me, Mrs Cairns," he said, and meant it. "That was utterly thoughtless of me. I should have known that your father would not enjoy an outing over rough roads. Perhaps I might entertain him some other way?" He'd had another idea. Possibly a better one. "Does he play cards, at all? Or chess, perhaps? I would be happy to offer him a game."

Lucy was drawing herself up in a way that suggested injured pride. She was touchy, his Lucy, when she thought she was being patronised.

"At your convenience, of course. And your father's. But if such a visit would be unwelcome, let my suggestion be forgotten."

Lucy seemed to soften a little. After all, she had agreed that Gabe could call on them, hadn't she? Though perhaps she hadn't expected his next visit to be quite so soon. "My father used to enjoy a game of chess, sir. But, now that he has difficulty in leaving the house, he does not have a regular opponent. I'm afraid it is not a game I ever learned, so I am of no use to him."

"From what I saw yesterday, Mrs Cairns, you are of a great deal of use to him," Gabe said, with feeling. "I am sure your father would say the same. Chess is a minor matter by comparison."

"Thank you, sir. You are very kind. And…and if you were to offer him a game of chess from time to time, here at home, he would be very grateful, I am sure. I know he misses it. He used to be a good player, I believe."

Gabe grinned. "Then I shall need to be on my mettle. I look forward to it. Er, when might it be convenient for me to call? To play chess with Mr Cairns, I mean?"

Lucy sighed. Her grip on the gate tightened a little but, in the end, she smiled up at him. "The day after tomorrow, perhaps, sir? You could come for dinner and play afterwards? He would like that, I am sure."

"I would like it, too. Very much. The day after tomorrow, then." He took up the reins again. Lucy would not want him to stay any longer, talking by the gate in full view of the whole village. "I wonder…"

"Yes, sir?"

Gabe chuckled. "I could not help wondering if there might be apple pie…"

# Chapter Nine

GABE SPENT THE INTERVENING day learning to master his tilbury and trying not to daydream about his darling Lucy. He thought of her as his darling, but did he have the right to? She had given no sign that she thought of him as other than her employer. Except…

Except there had been that moment, at the end of his first visit, when he'd offered to leave her strictly alone. She'd blushed and said—almost said—that she didn't want him to. Did that mean that she might have feelings for him? As a man, rather than as a master? As a potential lover, even?

He must assume nothing. And he must not risk upsetting her. He could hope, but that was all.

The tilbury horse was more difficult to control than the plodding beast for the gig, so Gabe soon had to focus all his attention on his driving. A good thing, he told himself, as he turned the tilbury onto the road to town. By the time he reached the main street, he reckoned he and the horse had reached a tolerable understanding.

Victorian Gabe's driving skills weren't too bad at all. Tomorrow he might even drive the tilbury out to Lucy's?

No. That would be showing off his wealth. It would remind her of the difference in their stations and that would be a very stupid thing to do. Much better to drive out in the homely gig.

Decision made, he turned the tilbury into the inn yard and handed it over to the ostler. Then he searched the shops until he found one that could sell him a chess board and pieces—a basic set, nothing fancy—and a couple of packs of playing cards. Mr Cairns might already have both, but Gabe would make him a gift of new ones, in return for the Cairns's generous hospitality. It wouldn't be wrong for him to do that, surely?

Would that be against the rules, too? He sighed. He hadn't a clue. Relaxed twenty-first century manners were so much easier to deal with than uptight Victorian propriety.

There was indeed apple pie for dinner. This time, though, Gabe refused Lucy's offer of a second helping. "I should dearly love another slice, Mrs Cairns, but I fear that, if I indulge my greed, I shall become too sleepy to offer your father a halfway respectable game of chess."

Andrew Cairns chuckled. "No danger there, sir. It do be a long while since I played. But with that fine new board, it will be a rare treat to have a game."

Lucy smiled at the mention of the new chess set.

Gabe smiled, too, pleased with his success there. He'd offered his gifts direct to Lucy's father, so that she would have no opportunity to refuse them.

And her father had accepted the modest tokens— especially the playing cards—with pleasure. "Just what we needed, sir. How did you guess? I been saying to

101

Lucy for a week now that we be needing new cards. Our old pack is all greasy. Not fit for a fine housekeeper to use." He referred to Lucy's new position with obvious pride.

Gabe would have preferred it if Cairns had said *not fit for a lady to use*. But Lucy was not a lady. Not yet. But she *had* been a lady—and a gentleman's wife—in that daguerreotype...

Lucy helped her father to his chair near the fire and began to clear the plates and cutlery from the dinner table.

"Let me help you with those, Mrs Cairns." Gabe gathered up the pie dish and the half-empty cream bowl. "Where should I put these?"

Lucy gasped. "No, sir. You must not. Indeed, you must not." She quickly put her crockery back onto the table and reached for the items Gabe was holding. "That is for me to do."

Her fingers touched his. And she flinched.

Gabe was unable to move. He could not let go of the crockery. All he could do was gaze into Lucy's face, desperately trying to read her expression. Had she felt what Gabe had felt? That shock of electricity running up his arm and kindling a pulsing glow throughout his body?

Predictably, she blushed rosily. His scrambled brain fancied—was he mistaken?—that her fingers trembled a fraction against the pie dish. For what seemed a long moment, she too stood unmoving, holding his gaze. And her eyes grew wide and dark. Then, blushing even redder, she looked away towards the fireplace and whispered, "If you please, sir. My father is waiting."

Gabe sighed and forced his body back under control. "As you wish, Mrs Cairns." With a wry smile, he left her to finish the clearing while he set about organising the chess game.

A small table and another chair were soon in place and the game began. Gabe knew he was not concentrating properly on his moves as the game progressed. He could not help it. Out of the corner of his eye, he kept catching glimpses of Lucy as she finished her chores. Eventually, she sat down in the rocking chair and began to do some household sewing. Mending a shirt, possibly. And she was studiously avoiding looking towards the chess players.

"Your move, Mr Bliss."

"Oh. I beg your pardon. I was miles away." Gabe moved a piece almost at random.

"Aye. I could see that. And still are, I'd say. Check."

At that, Lucy looked up from her stitching. When she saw that Gabe was watching her, rather than focusing on the chess board, she shook her head a little and bent to her work once more.

Gabe could feel his own colour rising in response. He had made a very careless move. He was about to lose his queen. And he didn't care. What mattered was that Lucy seemed concerned that he, Gabe, was failing to concentrate on what he should be doing, because he was dreaming about something else. Or someone else...

Was she beginning to realise how Gabe felt about her? Was she willing, perhaps, to return those feelings? He really, really hoped so. But, until he could find a way of being alone with her, he had no way of knowing. And, right now, he had run out of ideas for how he might engineer a tête-à-tête. All he could do was to keep visiting the cottage, on the pretext of playing chess with Lucy's father.

After Gabe made the only move available to him,

Cairns took his queen, with a gleeful chortle. "Mate in two, I reckons, sir."

"Good grief. So it is. Well played, Mr Cairns. Your daughter did warn me that you were a fine player. And you are."

The old man shook his head and smiled. "So are you, sir. Apart from that one careless move. P'raps next time, we should have our game *before* dinner?"

Gabe found himself smiling at that. "You are generous, sir. Let us agree to blame my poor play on your daughter's splendid cooking." He glanced across at Lucy who had looked up again at the sound of her name. "Your father has suggested a rematch, Mrs Cairns. And more of your excellent hospitality." He took a deep breath and decided to seize the opening that Lucy's father had given him. Tomorrow would be pushing it, but… "Would the day after tomorrow be suitable?"

For three more chess-playing visits, Gabe was unable to get a moment alone with Lucy. There had been glances, and blushes, certainly, but sadly—in Gabe's view—no more touching. Lucy had been particularly careful to avoid any risk of that. Gabe had recognised her game plan and gone along with it, knowing that if he was too bold, she might not let him visit again. In her father's house, she held all the cards.

When, on his fifth visit, Gabe did finally manage to persuade her to take a walk with him, it was awkward, even though they were not to go beyond the garden and the orchard. Lucy would not take his arm and kept a distance between them. She was clearly embarrassed and, he suspected, worrying that he might have lecherous designs on her, like Weir.

He took the issue head-on. "Please do not be

concerned, Lu— Er, Mrs Cairns. You are in no danger from me, I promise you. My intentions are honourable."

She stared at him, wide-eyed. "Honourable? I do not understand, sir. You are my employer."

"I am. And, in truth, I wish I were not. My intentions *are* honourable. I wish to court you, Lucy Cairns."

"Wh...wh...what? I...I beg your pardon. I must have misheard. Did you say—?"

"You did not mishear. I said I wished to court you. And I do. If you will allow me to do so."

"Oh." She rocked back on her heels. "That is impossible," she managed, at last. "You are a gentleman. I am a servant."

"And if I am happy to ignore the so-called gulf between us, would you not do so also, Mrs Cairns?"

A little smile flickered at the corner of her mouth. He suspected it was because he was still giving her the dignity of her full name and status.

"Thank you for that, sir," she said quietly. "Most employers would believe they had the right to presume. And yet it seems you do not."

He hated her use of "seems". Did she really not believe him? Did she not *want* to believe him? Whichever it was, he had to convince her. At this moment, it mattered more than anything. "No. I do not. You have the status of housekeeper. You are entitled to be called 'Mrs Cairns' and no one should address you by your given name unless you grant them leave. No one. Including me."

Her eyes warmed as she gazed up at him.

He had been right to follow his instincts. If he was going to woo Lucy Cairns, he would have to tread very carefully. And yet, that glow in her cheeks suggested she was not totally unwilling, however much she might protest about the difference in rank.

*Time to chance your arm, Gabe. You may never have another moment alone with her. Tell her now!*

"Mrs Cairns, would you permit me to continue to visit you here and to court you?"

She took a deep breath. She had gone a little pale. "A master courting a servant? It is not normal. And I have never heard of a case that was honourable," she added proudly. She shook her head and turned her back on him. She was clearly planning to return to the house and the safety of her father's chaperonage.

If she refused him now, Gabe might never have another chance to speak. She might forbid him the house. And he had to do it while she was here at home, in her father's house. It would be impossible to woo her once she returned to the Manor, as Gabe's servant. That *would* be dishonourable, for what choice would she have there? Accept her employer's advances or be thrown out on the street? At home, she had a real choice. And Gabe was desperate to hear that she would permit his advances.

"Mrs Cairns, my intentions *are* honourable, as I have already said," he began softly, addressing her stiff back. "I should like to court you, here at your father's house, and in the proper form. Exactly as I would court any lady. No matter how high her station."

Lucy turned slowly back to face him. She was even paler now. And her jaw was set. "There is a huge gulf between us, sir. And…you will excuse my plain speaking, I hope, but you leave me no choice, given what you have said. I could not—" She suddenly turned sheet white and stared down at her feet. Was she afraid to look him in the eye? Was she going to turn him away? "Sir, I am an honest, God-fearing woman, brought up to know what is right and what is wrong." Her voice sank to a whisper. It was so low and hesitant, it was difficult to make out her words. "I...I will not be any man's m–mistress."

Gabe stomach knotted as he realised what she was thinking. Had he hurt her? Insulted her, even? She did not believe him. She did not believe *in* him, or in his honour. That hurt *him*. A great deal. But his own feelings did not matter here. If he did not convince her now, this very moment, he would lose her. Completely. He could not bear the thought of that. "Mrs Cairns, I do not seek to make you my mistress," he said brusquely.

Her colour returned a little, but the look she threw him was still full of doubt. And embarrassment.

He realised immediately that his words had been bald and arrogant. He was sounding exactly like the tyrannical masters she had learned to avoid. It was no wonder that she still doubted him.

Gabe needed to do something to convince her of his sincerity. But what?

It was obvious, really.

He dropped to one knee on the muddy garden path. Lucy gasped and put out a shaky hand to wave him up again, but nothing was going to stop Gabe now. He knew he was doing the right thing, this time. He stayed exactly where he was, gazing up at her. "I love and admire you, Mrs Cairns. I seek to make you my wife. And, if you will permit it, I will ask your father's permission to make you an offer of marriage. May I do so?"

She hesitated visibly. She clasped her hands together. Was that to hide their shaking? Her wide and wondering eyes seemed to say "yes" to his proposal, but her reply—when it eventually came—was much less encouraging. "Please rise, sir. I cannot answer you if you are kneeling

107

in the dirt." When he reluctantly obeyed, she sighed deeply. "If I allow you to speak to my father, it must be on the understanding that if he refuses his permission, then I refuse also."

"So you do not wish to marry me, Mrs Cairns?" he said in a hoarse voice. He was having trouble keeping his emotions under control. He had played his last card. And Lucy was about to decide whether he would win or lose the game.

Except this was no game.

She looked away. "I…I did not say that. Not precisely. But I will not marry any man without my father's blessing."

"Ah, that I understand. And I respect you for it, Mrs Cairns. You will allow me to approach your father, then?"

"I…I…" She was blushing now. "Yes, sir. I will."

The glow began in his middle and seemed to spread through his whole body. Even his finger ends seemed to be tingling with the warmth of it. She was willing. He was sure of it. In that moment of triumph, he could not resist pushing his luck even further. "And do you also hope that I succeed with him, ma'am?"

The smile she gave him then was laced with a mixture of shrewd insight and exasperation. She raised her right hand to hold him off, though he had made no move to touch her. "My hopes, sir, are my own. I shall take a turn around the orchard now—alone—so that you and my father may conclude your discussions without me." She dropped him a dignified curtsey, turned her back and walked briskly down the path towards the apple trees.

"It is out of the question, sir." Andrew Cairns was sitting very straight in his place and glaring at Gabe.

108

"Why?" Gabe asked quietly.

Lucy's father spluttered a bit and then said, "Because you are her employer. Because you are a gentleman and Lucy is a cabinet-maker's daughter. Because... because it is not the way of things."

"Sir, I would not be the first gentleman to marry for love and to choose a woman that society did not approve of. Why, the Lord Chancellor himself eloped to Gretna Green with the woman he loved and he was a peer of the realm. I am nothing so high, only a simple country gentleman. Your daughter is a fine woman and will make me a fine wife. And, sir, I love her. I would not dishonour her by making her anything less than my lawful wife."

"Your proposal is honourable. That I do admit. Many a man of your station would try to make my poor girl his mistress. And then cast her aside when he was tired of her." He shook his head and snorted. "It has happened to many a serving wench, as the whole world knows. And the 'upright' gentlemen continue on their merry way until they light on the next girl to debauch."

"But I abhor such behaviour, sir. Surely you can see that?"

"Aye. Aye, I do. And I honour you for it, Mr Bliss. Yet..."

"And yet you will not give us your blessing?"

"I... Tell me, sir. What does my Lucy want? Does she understand how difficult such a union would be? Especially for her? 'Tis always the woman's part to suffer."

"I believe she does understand, sir. As do I. And I believe we are both ready for whatever might come to us if we marry. But we will not be wed without your blessing. She is adamant about that. And, however much

I love her, I accept it too. So the decision rests with you. But please believe that this is for her happiness."

"Hmm." The old man puffed on his pipe for several minutes.

Gabe said nothing. He knew he had to wait.

Finally, Andrew Cairns laid his pipe aside and smiled at Gabe. "Gabriel Bliss, I do accept that you love my daughter. And that you are an honourable man who wishes to make her as happy as her dear mother made me. You may offer for her with my good will, but the decision will be hers. If she do choose to accept you, I will give you both my blessing."

"Sir, I—"

"But if you do not love and protect her, as you must vow to do at the altar, I swear on my dear wife's memory that I will have my revenge on you, even if I has to haunt you from beyond the grave."

Gabe rose and bowed. "Sir, you have my permission to do that. For I will never, ever, give you cause."


"Mrs Cairns."

Lucy turned from where she was studying the bark of an old apple tree. Her expression was anxious, though she was trying to conceal it. And failing. Her eyes gave her away every time.

Gabe bowed. "Mrs Cairns, your father has given me permission to pay my addresses to you."

Lucy gasped, but her eyes were glowing.

"However, he has made clear that the decision rests with you. If you will have me—will you, dear Mrs Cairns?—he will give us his blessing." Gabe made to drop to his knees again but Lucy stopped him with a firm hand on his arm.

"I think," she said, smiling shyly, "that you should

110

call me 'Lucy' now, sir."

"Only if you call me by name, too. 'Gabriel' is my given name. Will you not use it, Lucy?"

She whispered it. Twice. And then she smiled up at him, confidingly. "Gabriel was an angel."

Gabe laughed. "I am no angel, Lucy, but if you will agree to marry me, I vow that I will do everything in my power to make you happy. Will you? Will you, my love?"

"Yes, Gabriel, I will," she responded firmly. His Lucy was a woman of decision.

He slid his hands round her trim waist and waited for her reaction. She did not shy away. She leant in to him and raised her smiling face to his. Expectantly?

Gabe had just enough self-control to say, "May I kiss you, Lucy?" His voice sounded strained in his own ears.

Her smile broadened. "I believe it is customary to seal a marriage bargain with a kiss," she said lightly. But her eyes were darkening as she spoke.

He bent his head and touched his lips to hers in a gentle kiss. He wanted more, but he hesitated to deepen the kiss. He must not frighten her.

Lucy responded by putting her arms round his neck and pulling him closer so that she could kiss him back. And there was an innocent passion in the way her lips explored his. It thrilled through Gabe's whole body. She did love him and she was trying to show it, even though she clearly had no experience of kissing a lover.

Gabe folded his arms round her and deepened the kiss, a very little. To his delight, Lucy moaned a little in her throat. And responded.

Their first kiss lasted a very long time. It sealed their bargain. And their love.

# Chapter Ten

"SIR. EXCUSE ME, BUT I feel I must ask. Is it indeed the case that you are to marry Cairns?"

Gabe felt a chill of fury shiver down his spine. "She is *Mrs Cairns* to you, Weir. And yes, she will be my wife, Mrs Bliss, and the mistress of this house, very soon."

The butler's face had gone almost as white as his crisp shirt. "If that is so, sir," he began, staring at a point somewhere over Gabe's head, "I must give warning. I could not serve under such a mistress."

"*Such a mistress?*" Gabe repeated in clipped tones. "Precisely *what* are you implying?"

"I imply nothing, sir. Anything I know to Mrs Cairns's, er, detriment, I have already shared with you. But such an unequal union is not seemly. Cairns—Mrs Cairns—is a mere servant. From the lower classes. A master may dally with a female servant if he feels the need to stoop, but a man of honour does not marry so far beneath him."

"Your idea of a master's honour is not mine, Weir," Gabe snapped.

He was having difficulty controlling his temper and suppressing his instinctive urge to wring the man's neck. "You may think it proper to *dally* and then discard, but I most certainly do not. Your desire to leave my service is noted. And approved."

"I shall be ready to leave at the end of the quarter, sir," Weir said stiffly.

"No, Weir. You will be ready to leave at the end of the week. At the latest."

The butler's eyebrows shot up.

"I will not retain a servant with such views for one day longer than necessary," Gabe said, with venom. "My wife-to-be is more than capable of running my household without a butler."

Weir had recovered himself a little. "She may find she is running your household without any staff at all, sir. I doubt that any of them will wish to remain." The unspoken words "to work under *such* a mistress" were left hanging in the air.

Gabe leaned forward very deliberately, put his elbows on the desk and clasped his hands so that he could rest his chin on them. He narrowed his eyes at the servant. The man was a self-righteous prig, without a doubt. He was everything that was wrong about the class system. On the one hand, he upheld it, insisting on his own dignities. On the other, he betrayed it by molesting defenceless women who should be under his benevolent care.

It was disgusting. And it was demeaning for Gabe to be associated with Weir in any way.

Gabe stared at the butler for a long time. He saw that it was making the man increasingly uncomfortable. Good. There was some obvious reddening on his neck, above that tight starched collar and neat bow tie. Had

Weir finally begun to realise what he was, and how much Gabe despised him?

"I think there is nothing more to be said, Weir. You may go."

The butler didn't move. "One question, if I may, sir?"

Gabe raised an eyebrow.

"What explanation am I to give to a future employer about my reason for leaving this house so suddenly? You will not wish me to share our differences over this matter, I take it?"

*Blackmailing bastard!*

Gabe dropped his hands to his lap and balled them into fists. Struggling for control, he took a long, deep breath and slowly blew it out through clenched teeth and lips that were threatening to curl into a snarl. "You will be paid until the end of the quarter. I suggest that you take a holiday, Weir. Forthwith. Your health does not prosper in this part of the country. Do I make myself clear? I will give you a character, with no mention of your insolent conduct towards my future wife. If I should be contacted by a prospective employer, I shall make no mention of anything to your detriment, to use your own phrase. That is more than you deserve."

Weir opened his mouth to reply but Gabe raised a hand to silence him. He was not finished yet. "However, if I am asked specific questions—about your conduct with female servants, for example—I shall answer them truthfully. You have been warned. Now, you may go."

The man seemed to have shrunk in his skin. He bowed shakily and left without another word.

Gabe collapsed back into his chair with a groan. Poor Lucy. What was he landing on her fragile shoulders? The servants would all give notice, probably. And the scandal of a master marrying one of his own maids would soon be the subject of avid gossip all over the county.

Once she was his lawfully-wedded wife, Lucy should be above such things but that was not the way of this class-ridden world. Society people—the ladies, especially—were likely to treat her with disdain, even contempt. He would not be able to shield her from all of it. Perhaps they should live abroad, at least for a space? Perhaps he should sell this house and move to somewhere they were not known?

It would depend on what Lucy wanted, he decided. For him, the difference in their stations was neither here nor there. She *said* she did not care about it, either, but when the poison-tongued harpies started their gossip, she might change her mind. He would need to be alert to that. And ready to do everything in his power to protect her.

Class differences must not be allowed to matter. He now knew, in his heart, that the only thing that mattered was love.

When Gabe voiced his fears to Lucy on their next walk in the orchard, he could hardly believe her reaction. She laughed. And then she reached up and kissed him.

"I am not afraid of what people may say, Gabriel. Not when I have you. And you were perfectly right that I can run your household. Of course I can. First thing tomorrow, I shall write to the agencies and organise interviews for new staff. It will not be so very difficult to replace those who choose to leave. You are known to be a good employer with a reputation for fairness. That counts for much. A master's reputation goes before him, you know. Servants gossip at least as much as their betters do."

"You are generous, Lucy. Especially about Weir,

after what he tried to do to you. I found I could not deny him a character, much though I might have wished to. It would have raised too much speculation about our marriage."

"No, it would have been unwise, I agree. Besides, if he had not tried to have me dismissed, we would not have found each other, would we?" She smiled mischievously at him. In that moment, he loved her more than ever. She was a total delight.

Gabe reached for her hand.

"In many ways, he has served you well," she continued thoughtfully, giving his fingers a quick caress. "He is no more of an autocrat than the average butler. He gives himself airs, but they all do. He is more honest than many. And he does not shut himself away in his pantry to get drunk on the master's wine, as so many butlers do."

Gabe's mouth twisted into a rueful smile. "There are clearly things I need to be wary of in hiring a new butler."

"If you would allow me to do that on your behalf, you might be spared some of those risks. Will you trust me to do it?"

"Of course I will. But it had better be as my wife that you do it. It is bad enough that we were living, unmarried, under the same roof for so long." He had done some researches in the household accounts and discovered that Lucy has been working for him for more than two years. It was sad that he could remember nothing of her before. He did not even know if they had spoken. Had he been kind to her? He hoped he had. When the time was right, he would be able to ask. But not yet.

Lucy's cheeks were glowing. It made her look

beautiful. And so very desirable.

Gabe swallowed. "I…I should like us to be married as soon as possible. Will you agree to that, Lucy?"

"It will cause a scandal. And the gossips will assume the worst." She shook her head for a second, gazing beyond the orchard into the middle distance. Then she seemed to make up her mind. "Well, let them. In nine months' time, the gossips will discover that they were wrong, will they not?"

It took Gabe a few seconds to catch up with Lucy's brutal logic. Yes, of course. The gossips would say that he had got one of his maids with child and was behaving more honourably to the woman than most masters would.

"But there will be scandal and gossip whatever we do," Lucy went on calmly. "So yes, let it be soon."

"Splendid. Once I have sorted matters at the Manor, I will go to London for a special licence. Today is Tuesday. If I leave early tomorrow, we could be married on… Hmm. Saturday? Can you be ready in so short a time, love?"

"Saturday? Yes. That will be perfect." She beamed at him. She was irresistible.

Gabe drew her into his arms and kissed her, long and thoroughly.

"Mmm. You are very persuasive, you know," she said, when they finally pulled apart. "Not that I needed persuading." She smiled mistily and touched a gentle hand to his cheek.

He could feel the calluses on her palm. From all that manual labour. From now on, though, she wouldn't have to lift a finger if she didn't wish to. And, while he was in London, he would seek out the best and most expensive hand cream available. Those calluses would soon be a

117

thing of the past. Hand cream would be only one of the many wedding presents he was planning to buy her. He was surprised by how much he was looking forward to giving her gifts.

She was still smiling at him. "Saturday can't come soon enough," she whispered, with a tiny tremor in her voice.

That was an extremely forward thing for an unmarried lady to say. And Gabe loved her for it. "For both of us," he agreed softly, and began to kiss her again.

# Chapter Eleven

ONCE CHARLES HAD CLEARED away the remnants of their light wedding-night supper and closed the door carefully behind him, Gabe reached across the table to take Lucy's hand. "That was a delicious meal, Mrs Bliss. Thank you."

"And I didn't have to cook it, either." She smiled mischievously at him.

He chuckled. "I'm glad Weir was wrong. Actually, I'm not really surprised that so many of the servants have decided to stay. They are more than ready to work for you, I think."

"It's early days, Gabriel. Things may change."

"Well, if they do, if anyone in this house should fail to give you the respect you are entitled to, you have my permission to dismiss them on the spot."

She nodded thoughtfully. She clearly knew that dismissals might be necessary in order to assert her authority as mistress. "But, if I have to do that, I may still give them a character?"

That made him smile. He squeezed her hand and

lifted it to his lips for a kiss. His Lucy would never forget that a servant's life could be precarious. And she would not inflict penury on anyone, however impudent they might be. "Lucy, my love, you are mistress here now. You will run our house exactly as you please. And if you choose to give an upstart servant a reference, that is for you to decide."

"Thank you, Gabriel. You are a good master."

"But I am not *your* master," he protested hotly. It might not be the Victorian way, but he wanted a marriage of equals. "You are my wife. We are partners. In everything, I hope."

She blushed and fixed her gaze on their clasped hands. What on earth was the matter? As his wife, she no longer had any cause for embarrassment.

Oh yes, she had. Was she remembering the night to come? He must not forget that his Lucy was totally inexperienced. In her virgin imaginings, Gabe's *everything* might be scary. Did she even know what husband and wife did together in bed?

He rose and gently pulled her up from her chair and into his arms. "I love you, Mrs Bliss," he whispered and kissed her before she had a chance to say a word in reply.

She did not resist. In fact, she kissed him back with even more passion than she had shown when they kissed in the orchard. She was his wife now, relaxed and confident in his arms. She did not seem at all afraid of what was to come.

Gabe's body responded instantly to Lucy's passion. He wanted her. Now. So very much. He deepened the kiss and dug his fingers into her beautiful fair hair. He could not resist her and she, it seemed, wanted him too.

It was the pinging sound of hairpins hitting the

parquet floor that brought them to their senses.

"Oh, goodness," Lucy cried, putting her hands to her tumbled hairstyle. She dropped to the floor and started scrabbling around for her hairpins. "Whatever will the servants think?"

"If they know what's good for them, they will not think anything, because they will not be around to see."

She had moved to the mirror above the fireplace and was trying desperately to restore her hair to its normal neatness.

He went to stand behind her and smiled at their combined reflections. "We are newly married, Mrs Bliss. We know that, and so do they. I imagine they will have retired to the servants' hall to drink our health."

"Really?"

Gabe allowed himself a smug smile. "I did suggest that they might. As soon as supper was over. With my wine, of course."

Lucy shook her head but she was beaming at him, nonetheless. "I should have known. You are a kind man, Gabriel Bliss, but devious with it."

He took that as a compliment. "Thank you, wife of mine. And now, um, it is getting late. Perhaps you would like to go up?" He swallowed hard, trying to sound matter-of-fact. "I will join you in half an hour or so. Will that be long enough, do you think?"

She could not look at him. And it seemed she could not speak, either.

She nodded swiftly, gathered up the rest of her pins and fled.


Having paced the dining parlour for twenty-five interminable minutes, Gabe couldn't wait any longer. As he had expected, no servants were to be seen in the hallway or in the corridor to his study where his wedding-night gifts were awaiting collection.

With the jewel case in his pocket and the ice bucket and glasses clutched against his chest, he took the stairs three at a time. His candle flickered dangerously in the draught but he ignored it. There were lit candles in the wall sconces. If his own candle went out, it wouldn't matter. He could light it again before he went into his bedchamber.

*Their* bedchamber.

Or perhaps Lucy would prefer darkness for her first time? That sudden thought made him stop dead on the threshold.

He must not get this wrong.

He blew out his candle and set it down on the table by the bedroom door.

This must be Lucy's choice.

Opening the door softly, he crept inside. The curtains were tightly drawn. The fire had almost burnt down in the grate, so there was precious little light from there. A single candle was lit, but it was on the table on Gabe's side of the huge bed. Lucy was lying on the far side, straight and rigid as a laid-out corpse, with the sheets pulled up to her chin.

*She even knows which side of the bed I sleep on.*

That absurd thought jolted him for a second. Then he realised. She had been a maid in his house. She had probably changed the linen on this bed many times. Of course she knew which side he slept on.

He set the ice bucket and the glasses beside the candle. Champagne might relax her, but it was too soon to open it. He kicked off his evening shoes and padded round the bed so that he could stand on Lucy's side and gaze his fill.

Her beautiful hair was loose on the pillow. Had she done that for him? Because she knew he loved to run his fingers through it?

Resisting the urge to touch her, he said gently, "Lucy, my love, may I sit here?"

She was startled by his request, but she moved across a little, to make room for him. Unfortunately, the bed linen still covered her completely, even when he sat on it.

He leaned forward and touched her cheek, ever so gently. And then dropped an equally gentle kiss on her lips. That made her smile up at him. And he fancied that her body was not quite so rigid any more. "Darling, I have brought champagne." He nodded towards the far side of the bed. "It is traditional for a wedding night."

"Is it?" she whispered.

"So I am told. Not having been married before, I cannot speak from experience."

She giggled nervously.

"May I pour you a glass, love? It might relax us both." When she did not reply, he went on lightly, "A wedding night can be scary, you know. For the husband as well as the wife. I might need Dutch courage. What if I were to fail to, er, to come up to scratch?"

She laughed then, a genuine laugh.

Now was the moment.

He pulled the case from his pocket. "It is also traditional for a husband to give his new wife a gift of love. I hope you like it. I was trying to match the blue of your eyes." He opened the case so that she could see the sapphire pendant with its sunburst surround of baguette diamonds. Even in the dim light, the stones glowed with mysterious fire.

Those beloved blue eyes widened and darkened.

123

"Oh," she breathed. "Oh, it is beautiful, Gabriel. Exquisite."

"May I put it on for you, love?" He extracted it from the box as he spoke.

"Now? In bed?"

"Why not? I'd like to know if I have chosen well. And the only way to judge is to see it hanging round the neck of the woman I love. Will you sit up a little, please, darling? I wouldn't want to catch the clasp in your hair." He was trying to keep his words unthreatening and unemotional. It was not easy.

"I... I..." She didn't move. Then, at last, she seemed to reach a decision. She swallowed hard and sat up.

The sheet slid down to the top of her breasts.

Gabe realised then that Lucy's shoulders were naked. And every inch of visible skin was blushing. The rosy colour seemed to continue down below the sheet. Were her breasts blushing too? And were they equally naked?

Suddenly, Gabe's evening breeches were much too tight. Coming up to scratch was no longer in doubt.

He gulped, trying to think of something to say that would not scare her. And would not betray how aroused he was.

"You will be wondering..." Her voice cracked. She cleared her throat and started again. "About..." She touched the burning skin at the base of her neck. "I had no suitable nightrail, you see, and I could not wear my old worn flannel for this—" The words all came out in a rush and then stopped dead.

Bless her. She was worrying that she had no proper trousseau. But he had hardly given her the time to assemble anything, had he? Now, as his wife, she could buy the finest, flimsiest fripperies to wear to his bed. He would encourage that. And enjoy the results, he was sure. For now, though, she needed reassurance.

And love.

He put his hand to her cheek and stroked gently. "So you chose to come to our wedding bed as God made you. Darling Lucy, thank you. Your trust is the greatest gift you could have given me."

She sighed deeply. And then she smiled up at him and lifted her hair so that he could fasten the jewel round her neck.

"It looks exactly right, love. Almost as beautiful as the woman wearing it. Would you like to see?" He fetched the hand mirror from the dressing table and gave it to her.

Her smiled broadened as she looked at her reflection. Then she tried to suppress it. "Vanity is a sin. I should not..."

"In that case—" he took the mirror and laid it on the table beside her "—you had better stop admiring yourself. Let me do it for you, instead." He gazed at her again, lovingly, to show that he meant it.

"Gabriel Bliss, you are—"

"Hmm? I am...?"

She took a deep breath. "I think you are wearing too many clothes," she said, blushing scarlet at her own daring, but refusing to look away this time.

"Are you sure, love? Do you know, er...? I mean, about..." He gestured vaguely in the direction of the bed.

Her blush subsided. "I am a country girl, Gabriel. I know how things are between male and female." She sounded confident. Until she added, with a nervy laugh, "In theory, at least."

"And you will allow me to put the theory to the test? Tonight?"

By way of answer, she reached up to put her hands

round his neck. The sheet fell to her waist. She was, indeed, proudly and beautifully naked. And she wanted him. If there had been any doubt about that, her long passionate kiss dispelled it.

Champagne forgotten, Gabe threw off his clothes and climbed into bed beside his wife.

And to his joy, she came willingly into his arms, turning her face up for his kiss.

He tried not to pull her too close to his naked body. What if his arousal frightened her? But it was no use. His Lucy wanted to be close to him, skin against skin, and she was trying to brush her legs against his. She succeeded.

But she did gasp, a very little, when she felt the length and strength of his erection against her naked belly.

There was nothing Gabe could say. He laid his fingers on one naked breast, stroking and caressing. Her nipple rose against his fingers. Too, too tempting. He dipped his head so that he could kiss and suckle her there. She flinched a little, but only at first. Soon she was moaning with the pleasure of it. As was he.

"Will you touch me, too, love?" he asked softly, raising his head and taking her hand in his. He was waiting for her response. She needed to be willing.

"Is…is that allowed?" she whispered.

Gabe didn't laugh. This was serious. "My darling, everything between a husband and wife is allowed, provided only that it gives us both pleasure. You may do with me precisely as you wish."

"Oh." She would not look at him, but she did put hand on his chest and slowly, slowly run it down to his belly. This time her "Oh," was longer and contained something that he suspected might be wonder. "You are so…so hard. And yet so soft. I did not imagine—" She stopped short and hid her face against his chest.

Gabe covered her fingers with his and encouraged her to grasp him fully.

"I–I won't hurt you, will I?"

"No, love," he chuckled. "No. Your touch is wonderful."

She was quickly becoming less shy and more adventurous. It took only one more invitation for her to start moving her hand on his erection.

He groaned. He couldn't help it.

"I *am* hurting you."

"No, my sweet. Not at all. You make me feel… Well, the only thing that would feel even more pleasurable would be if I were inside you."

"Oh." Soft and long drawn-out. "Is that what you want, Gabriel? Now?"

"It is what I want. What I long for. But not until you are ready, my darling. Will you let me touch you?" Returning his mouth to her breast, he ran his hand down her flank and across the top of her thigh to the core of her. She did not resist at all. She even relaxed against his fingers. He stroked gently. Once and again. She was hot, and wet. She was ready. He hoped. "I want you, sweetheart," he said hoarsely.

"I want you, too," she whispered back.

He settled into the cradle of her hips, still kissing her breast. And then he returned to kissing her luscious mouth. Deeply, passionately, teasing her dancing tongue with his own. "Do you trust me, love?" he managed, between kisses.

"Yes, Gabriel. I trust you. And I love you."

That was enough. A moment later, they were joined, fully and completely.

Lucy gasped a little.

"Did I hurt you, darling? I am so sorry."

"N–no. Not…not really. I… Ooh," she moaned as he moved a little within her, settling deeper. That didn't sound like a gasp of pain. But was it pleasure?

Gabe managed to stay still within her. He had to be sure.

"Don't stop now. I want you. All of you."

"Oh, my love," he moaned against her cheek. "My darling wife." He started to thrust again, more strongly now. Faster. Harder.

And then, it was over. The ecstasy of release flooded his body. It was unlike anything he had ever experienced. This—this was real love. And, now, they were truly man and wife. The joy of it fizzed through him.

Until he realised what he had done. And not done.

He had been much too quick, unable to control his desire for her. He had made Lucy his wife, but he had failed to satisfy her.

Lucy did not seem to think that. She nestled into the crook of his shoulder and dropped a teasing kiss on his nipple.

But he had not satisfied her. He had failed there. Still, there were other ways. He ran his hand down her thigh again and started to touch her, with soft stroking motions.

"Gabriel, what…?"

He did not let her finish. He started kissing her again, instead. And moments later, gloriously, joyously, she groaned into his mouth as her whole body shuddered, again and again. He wrapped his arms rounds her and drew her close until he could feel the rapid beating of her heart and her quick breaths against his skin. He said nothing, waiting. He had given her fulfilment. Later, he hoped to make it even better.

"I...I have never felt that before," she managed at last. "It was... Oh, Gabriel, it was wonderful."

Gabe smiled against her cheek. "It is one of the pleasures of being husband and wife, love."

"Really? Can we do it again?"

That made him laugh out loud. Lucy's theory of sex did not, apparently, cover what a man's body could and could not do. And how soon. "Not yet, I'm afraid. Later. When I have recovered a little."

"Oh." She sounded disappointed.

Gabe wanted to crow with delight. What a wife he had found. She loved him. And she would become a bedmate in a million. But he did not say so. It was too soon. Instead, he asked the question that had been on the tip of his tongue for ages. "When did you first think you could love me, Lucy darling?"

"The first time you were kind to me. It must be two years ago, now."

"Really? Remind me. What did I do?" He had no idea how he had treated her, but he was anxious to learn more.

"I'm not surprised you don't remember. I was only a new maid, after all. We were here in this bedchamber. I had spilled your morning hot water. Mr Weir was berating me and you made him stop. You said that anyone could make such a mistake, especially a poor girl carrying a can of water that was much too heavy for her to manage."

She sighed, seeming to remember. "I admired you then. You were kind and generous to me. And I saw that you acted with the same generosity to other servants. It was only admiration, I assure you. I did not dare to think

129

of anything beyond that. Anything more was an idiotic dream."

"And you, Lucy dearest, are never idiotic, are you?"

"I try not to be."

He smiled down at her. "Where would you like to go for our honeymoon? The whole of Europe is at your feet. Or the rest of this country, if you prefer. We could travel for a few months, perhaps? It would allow us to get to know each other better. And for the gossip here to die down. A bit, at least."

"It will never die down completely, Gabriel. Country gentleman marries downstairs maid? That story will run and run."

"I fear you are right. But what if we lived abroad? We could do that. Or move to another part of the country. I have not owned this house for all that long. I could easily sell up and move elsewhere. Somewhere we are not known. Somewhere where you would not be the target of malicious gossip."

She shook her head. "The gossip will follow us, wherever we settle. And we should not let the gossips think we are running away. We have the right to hold our heads up, wherever we are. We have done nothing wrong."

"Apart from falling in love?"

"That can never be wrong, Gabriel. We love each other. We want each other. What more need be said?" She ran her hand over his taut belly and began to tickle his balls. She was a very fast learner, his Lucy.

To Gabriel's surprise, his body responded. He blew out a long and rather shaky breath. "It seems you will have your wish, Mrs Bliss. You did say, didn't you, that you wanted to do it again?"

She beamed at him.

Her eyes were twinkling in the half-light. "I did. And I do."

When Gabe woke up, he refused to open his eyes. He wanted to stay in dreamy darkness. He wanted to relish the moment, his first morning as a married man, husband to his darling Lucy. She was his now, fully his, but he still longed to touch her, to taste her, to breathe in the glorious scent of her hair. There would be plenty of time, later, to gaze at her and marvel at the beauty which had blossomed since he put his ring on her finger. For now, touch was so much more important. He reached across the bed to stroke her skin.

She wasn't there.

That jerked him fully awake. Where was she?

It was still dark. It must be very early. He couldn't see a thing. But he could hear someone moving in the room.

He recognised that soft step. Lucy. She had simply left their bed for a moment. Perhaps to answer a call of nature? No doubt she would return to him soon.

But Gabe was too impatient to wait.

"Lucy, darling, come back to bed."

# Chapter Twelve

"LUCY, DARLING, COME BACK to bed."

*What?* Lucy stopped in her tracks. She couldn't believe what she was hearing. Gabriel Bliss—working man's champion and prize idiot—was calling her "Lucy". Not only that, he was calling her "darling". And inviting her into his bed.

*Back* into his bed?

That concussion had clearly shaken up his brain. Gabe would never say such a thing if he was in his right mind. He was probably sound asleep; dreaming.

But he seemed to be dreaming about being in bed with Lucy. And making love with Lucy? She shivered in the darkness. It was not an unpleasant vision, but an impossible one, given Gabe's stubborn insistence on sticking to his blasted principles.

She crept closer to the bed, shading her little torch with her hand. She didn't want to disturb his sleep. It wasn't even six o'clock. It would be dark for hours yet.

She had been tossing and turning all night, worrying

about Gabe. On her earlier visit, around two in the morning, she'd even risked shining her torch on his face. He had seemed to be peacefully asleep. But that was then. Now, since he was dreaming—and talking in his sleep, too—he might be on the verge of waking up.

Should she wake him?

No. The doctors had said he had to be careful. And to rest. A shock, she was sure, would be bad for him after that blow on the head. How would he cope if she woke him up from the middle of a dream where he thought he was in bed with her?

Actually, it was tempting. If she sat on the bed beside him and whispered his name, would he take her in his arms? Would he continue to live his dreams? And let her join him in them?

Mmm. Deep in her gut, warmth began to unfurl. Her body wanted her to try.

Unfortunately, her conscience intervened. Sternly. Gabe was a guest in her house and a recovering invalid. She might get a sexy frisson out of her mad plan, but what would Gabe get? A terrible guilt trip, probably, the moment he woke up properly. And in his current weakened state, that would not only be unfair, it might do lasting damage. He must be left to sleep, whatever was happening in his dreams.

She made for the door, rather than the bed. There would be other opportunities, once Gabe was fully recovered. Now that she knew, for sure, that he *did* fancy her, she would not fail to take them. And she could make opportunities of her own, if she had to.

"I give you fair warning, Gabriel Bliss," she whispered, in a voice so low that he couldn't possibly hear, even if he was fully awake. "I *will* be in your bed. But later. Not now. Later, when you're better." With the greatest care, she turned the handle, opened the door and crept out on silent feet.

It was already light when Lucy went back to Gabe's room, carrying a cup of tea as an excuse for visiting him. She knocked softly and waited.

Silence.

Hmm. She put an ear to the door. She couldn't hear a thing but that might be simply because the door was thick mahogany. Or perhaps Gabe was up, and in the bathroom? Either that or he was still sound asleep. If he was awake he would have responded to her knock, wouldn't he?

She reminded herself that he had gone to bed in pyjamas. So she was unlikely to embarrass him by catching him naked. Just to be sure, though, she knocked again.

Another silence.

Very softly, she turned the handle and peeked into the room. Yes, he was still in bed. He hadn't moved at the sound of the door opening so he was probably still sleeping. That would do him good. The doctor had recommended it. So Lucy would steal in and put the tea on the bedside table where he would see it when he woke up. It would soon go cold, of course, but she could always come back with a fresh cup in half an hour.

The room was gloomy. The curtains were closed and the half-hearted December light wasn't penetrating very far. Still, Lucy could see well enough to ensure she didn't trip over anything.

She crept across to the side of the bed and looked down at his sleeping face. Relaxed, he was handsomer, certainly much more attractive than when he was growling at Lucy for being the boss's daughter.

Lucy made space on the bedside table and set the cup down. Unfortunately, it clinked in its saucer.

"Lucy? Lucy, you'll freeze out there. Come back to bed."

*What? Still dreaming?*

But this time, Gabe had moved. He was awake. Or nearly.

"I've brought you a cup of tea, Gabe," Lucy said, as calmly as she could.

"But we have servants to do—" His eyes opened wide and he stared up at Lucy's face. His gaze was unfocused. He looked stunned.

Oh dear. The concussion was still affecting him.

They seemed to stare at each other for ages. And then his left hand came out from under the bedclothes and he ran his fingers down his cheek. He frowned. He seemed to be surprised, for some reason. And puzzled rather than annoyed.

Lucy had no idea what was going on, except that Gabe was still unwell and she needed to take care of him. "I don't know how much you remember, Gabe, but you had a bad concussion. Dad and I are looking after you at the Manor House. And the doctors said you have to rest until the dizziness and confusion have cleared up. I suggest… If you'd rather go back to sleep, I'll take the tea away." She paused, waiting for a response.

Gabe simply went on staring at her. It wasn't hostile. It was definitely dazed.

Eventually, to break the silence, Lucy said, "Do you still have a headache?"

He gave a little groan. "N–no. No, not really."

"Well, that's progress," she said, in a bracing voice. "That's excellent. Perhaps a cup of tea—I put three sugars in it—will make you feel even better?"

135

"I don't like sugar in my tea, Lucy. You know that. You've waited on me often enough."

"Have I?" she said, surprised.

"Sorry, I didn't mean… Sorry, I… It was…"

"Don't try to explain," Lucy said kindly. "Look, if you hate the idea of sugar, I'll fetch you another cup. But in an hour or so, eh? When you've had a little more sleep?"

"Yes. Thank you, Lucy. You're very kind."

Lucy retrieved the tea and tiptoed out before he could remember that he did not allow himself to call her by her first name.

Back in the corridor, with the door firmly shut between them, she gave a single little crow of triumph. One step forward. And she didn't intend that there would be any steps back.


Gabe closed his eyes and kept them tightly shut, hoping the confusion would go away. It didn't.

Actually, he could do with a cup of tea. It might clear his head. Automatically, he reached for the bell pull by the bed.

There was no bell pull.

His arm collided, instead, with a lamp on the table. A standard, modern, electric light. He was back in his world—what he had to call his *real* world—and his idyll with Lucy was over.

Something knotted and griped in his stomach.

He put a shaky hand to his cheek again. No, he hadn't been mistaken. The Victorian side-whiskers were gone. There was a couple of days' stubble on his chin, but that was it. How long was it since he'd been hit by the cedar? Two days? He wasn't quite sure. And he needed to check what kind of state he was in.

He forced himself to sit up and swing his legs out of

the bed. He was slightly woozy. He took a few long, deep breaths and waited for the room to stop going round and round. Then he got up and half-walked, half-stumbled towards the bathroom.

At the end of the bed, he stopped. He steadied himself on the bedpost. And then he looked at the room. Really looked. It was the same room.

But it wasn't the same. All the furniture was different. His room with Lucy—Lucy, his darling wife—had been over-decorated and very plush. A hundred and fifty years on, the same room was neat and rather spare, with furniture that was all clean lines and simplicity. He had always preferred the Scandinavian look to chintz and twee nostalgia. And yet he was missing the over-furnished Victorian room with his marriage bed.

Not to mention his beloved bride.

Would he ever get over losing her?

In the bathroom, he checked his face in the mirror. He was pretty bruised, though the bruises were mostly purple now, rather than black, which meant he was improving. He ought to have a shave, but he didn't have the energy. Instead, he splashed some cold water on his face and staggered back to bed. Just those few steps had exhausted him.

He ought to have fallen asleep again at once, but he couldn't. Part of his brain was wrestling with the memory of his lost marriage dream. Like a dog with a meaty bone, his brain positively refused to let it go. It had been just a dream, hadn't it? And yet it had been so real. And consistent, too. Dreams tended to jump about all over the place, but his dream of Lucy had not. It had started in one place and time, and had continued in the same place and time. Everything had been consistent and real and chronological. Right up to the point where he woke up on the morning after their wedding and found Lucy had left their bed.

Dreams didn't work that way, surely? So was it something else, a glimpse of a previous life for both of them?

Impossible. There was no such thing as reincarnation. Or time travel. His vision, or whatever it was, must have been the result of the concussion. He had come to bed with scrambled brains and, in his troubled sleep, he had had a remarkable dream. It couldn't be anything more than that.

Could it?

But the daguerreotype he'd seen in the museum had been of himself and Lucy. That was where it had all started.

And that was *before* the storm.

Gabe didn't know how to deal with that, so he deliberately parked it in his mental pending tray. He needed more sleep. His brain wasn't up to working through difficult puzzles. He'd do better once he was properly rested.

He made himself more comfortable and closed his eyes.

As he was drifting off, a new idea came to him. Yes. Of course. He would visit the museum and ask Alice to show him the daguerreotype again. He had the strangest feeling about that shape-shifting image of himself and his darling Lucy. Somehow it would resolve things for him. Once and for all.

"Jane? It's Lucy."

"Oh, hi, Lucy. What can I do for you? Are you coming over to the shop?"

"Is Gabe there?"

"No, he's gone to town. To the museum, he said. But I can tell him—"

"No, please don't. I don't want him to know I'm phoning you."

"Why ever not?"

Lucy took a deep breath to calm her jangling nerves. "I wanted to ask you to keep an eye on him. And I don't want him to know I've asked. That's why I couldn't come to the shop. In case he saw me and wanted to know what I was doing there."

"Fair enough. But what's worrying you? He seems pretty OK to me. You and your father obviously did a grand job of looking after him. There's hardly a bruise to be seen now and he says he's as right as rain."

"I'm not sure what it is. I can't put my finger on it. But I know there's something wrong. It's the way he keeps looking at me. As if he can't quite place me. But that makes no sense. We've known each other since we were kids, so why on earth is he looking at me as if I'd grown horns? To be honest, I blame the concussion. I don't think he can be fully recovered."

"That *is* odd. And you may be right. In fact, he…"

Lucy waited, but Jane didn't finish whatever she'd been going to say. "What has he done?" she prompted. "You know you can tell me, Jane."

"Well, not *done*, exactly. He's been very grumpy, that's all. I asked him to come to us again for Christmas day and he refused. He'd rather stay here in the flat alone—with a microwave dinner for one. Said 'all that ho-ho-ho-ing' isn't his thing. In fact, he said he hates Christmas and he'll be very glad when it's all over."

"Wow! He really gave you an earful, didn't he?"

"I put it down to him having a sore head. But I won't ask again. I don't think he really enjoyed Christmas with us last year. I can see that now. Christmas is a family thing and he doesn't have any. Maybe that's why he hates it?"

"Maybe. But it's not like Gabe to be so rude, is it?"

"Oh, no, he wasn't rude. He thanked me for inviting him and all that. Very politely. It's just that he was very firm about refusing. And about hating Christmas." Jane sighed. She loved having all her family round her at Christmas.

"He does sound like a bear with a sore head," Lucy agreed. "And now I come to think of it, why has he gone to the museum when he'd normally be getting the Christmas stock ready in the nursery? He does seem to be behaving a bit strangely, doesn't he?"

"Mmm."

"So do you think you could keep an eye on him? Discreetly? If there's anything else that worries you—anything at all—give me a call and I'll come over. If I have to, I'll strongarm him into Maisie and take him back to the doctor's myself."

Jane chortled. "Good luck with that, Lucy. He's bigger and stronger than you, or hadn't you noticed?"

"I'll find a way. I'll get Muffin to bite his ankles if I have to. So will you do it for me, Jane? Please?"

"I trust your instincts, lovey. So yes, I will. I'll tip you the wink if I see anything odd. I promise. OK?"

"You're a star, Jane. Thank you. And if Gabe had any sense—which we both know he hasn't—he'd thank you, too."

It wasn't the same image.

Gabe stared and stared but the daguerreotype stubbornly refused to offer him the picture he'd seen before. It showed him the Manor and a nineteenth-century man and woman standing in front of it, but they weren't Gabe and Lucy. There was a vague likeness—he was tall and dark, and she was fair—but that was all.

He went to find Alice again. "Are you sure that's the same daguerreotype I saw in the exhibition? It looks, er, different."

"Trick of the light, probably." Alice smiled indulgently. "But I can guarantee it's the same daguerreotype you saw before. We only have the one. And we're lucky to have that."

"Oh. I see."

But he didn't.

He went back to the research room and studied the image more closely. Maybe Alice was right. In the exhibition, the light had been dim. Here, it was brighter. He couldn't doubt what he was seeing now. Had his mind been playing tricks on him that first time? Showing him Lucy, and himself, in the image because that was what he *wanted* to see?

Maybe it was simply that he'd been obsessing about Lucy back then? He certainly was now. That Victorian marriage might have been a hallucination but it felt totally real, even here in the museum with the original image in front of him. Gabe knew that, if he closed he eyes, he'd be able to taste his Lucy. And touch her. He'd loved and desired her in his dream and he—

His head started throbbing again. He shouldn't have come. It was too soon after his concussion and he was having difficulty in thinking straight. One thing he did know. He needed to stop dwelling on his weird Victorian mirage.

And he needed to stop tormenting himself about Lucy Cairns.

141

# Chapter Thirteen

LUCY WAS GOING THROUGH the list of people who'd signed up for the next day's drag hunt. It wasn't the first of the year—they'd had a couple in November and they'd both gone very well—but Pat's list of participants was much longer than on the previous occasions. Pat, being the super-efficient PA she was, had provisionally booked extra marshals and left all the details on Lucy's desk. All Lucy had to do was email or text the marshals to confirm that they were definitely needed. And that they would be paid by the Manor estate.

The phone rang. Lucy answered in her usual businesslike manner.

"Hi," said a familiar voice. Still not using her name, of course. "It's Gabe."

What on earth was he phoning her for? He never phoned her. She felt her pulse quickening, a very little. "Hi, Gabe. What can I do for you?"

"I, er, I wondered if you'd like to come out for a drink." He paused. Lucy thought she heard him swallow, but she couldn't be sure. "There's something I'd like to discuss with you. On neutral ground, as it were."

Oh. Business. For a second she'd thought he might actually want her company. For herself. She should have known better.

"Sure," she said lightly. "I'm free this evening, as it happens. What about you?"

"Oh. Oh, well, yes. Tonight would be great. Meet you in *The Feathers*, about seven?"

"Fine, I'll be there."

"Good. See you then. Bye." He hung up. Just like that. The whole conversation—except it hadn't been a conversation, not really—had lasted less than a minute. Typical.

She should have been cross with him, but she found herself wondering what his new proposition might be. Something to do with the nursery, of course, but was there a place for her in it? Why did he want to discuss it with her rather than her father?

A little voice piped up that maybe business was an excuse. Maybe Gabe had wanted to ask Lucy out but his courage had failed him at the last minute? So he'd turned a date into a business meeting instead?

Possible, but unlikely, she decided. And she certainly wasn't going to pin her hopes on a fantasy like that. She would meet him in the pub, as arranged, and she would expect him to have a new scheme to present to her. If there was more to it, well, she'd think about that when—and if—it ever happened. Chances were it wouldn't.

Not with Gabriel Class-Warrior Bliss.

"Lucy?"

She was jerked back to the present. "Oh, hi, Dad. Didn't expect to see you again till later. Weren't you going across to the building site?"

He chuckled. "You've lost track of time, my girl. I've already done that. It didn't take long. There was nothing for me to do there. Everything's under control. For once, we're ahead of schedule." He shook his head, smiling. "Amazing, considering it's December."

Lucy grinned back at him. "You've been really lucky with the weather, since that huge storm. Though if it starts tipping it down, your precious schedule might well go pear-shaped."

"True. So I'd better not tempt fate. It might snow." He turned away and stared at the portrait above the fireplace for a long time.

Lucy saw that there was a strange little smile curling the edge of his mouth. She knew that smile. It meant her father was plotting something. No point in asking what it was, though. He wouldn't confide in Lucy until he was good and ready.

She waited, wondering what he was up to.

Eventually he turned back to her and said, "I've been thinking about Christmas, Lucy."

That wasn't good. Lucy's mother had died on Christmas Eve. It was a time when sad memories haunted both of them. That was one reason why they always tried to fill the house with guests over the festive period. They had never discussed it openly—the wound was still too raw, even after fifteen years—but they had come to an unspoken understanding that the solution to their mutual problem was to hold a Boxing Day shoot and to invite the guns and their partners to spend Christmas at the Manor as well. When Lucy and her father were both running round after their guests, and trying to sell antiques to them while they were at it, there was very little time to indulge in painful memories. And since the traditional Boxing Day hunt also started from the Manor, the two of them rarely had time to catch their breath over the holiday period. As a strategy, it had worked pretty well for the last five years.

"I've been thinking it's time I stopped mourning your mother," Sir Drew said, thoughtfully.

Lucy's stomach turned somersaults. Was he thinking of getting married again? If so, he'd been remarkably secretive about his new woman. She held her breath, waiting for whatever would come next.

"I need to celebrate what we had together," Sir Drew went on, glancing back round at the portrait. "We had a wonderful marriage. We had you. I still have you, of course. As well as all those happy memories. So I've decided to create something special, as a sort of thank-you to Margaret."

No new wife, then. Deep in her heart, Lucy was glad, though she knew she was being selfish. She ought to want her father to find happiness again—and she did, she really did—but she wasn't sure whether she could welcome another woman in her mother's place. For the moment at least, it seemed that she wouldn't have to try.

"I've found a very interesting young goldsmith. He's got a fantastic eye and some really innovative ideas. Anyway, he's designed me a special ring, with our initials, M and A, entwined through ivy leaves." He held up his right hand and waggled his little finger. "I'll wear it here. I wouldn't want it on my other hand." He had never stopped wearing the plain gold wedding band on his left hand. Lucy was sure he never would.

"That sounds wonderful, Dad. Can I see the design?" She got up from her chair.

"It's on my computer. I'll show you in a minute, if you like. The thing is, I want it to be made from your mother's wedding ring and so the goldsmith needs to know how much gold there is in it. I can't imagine it weighs much; she had such slender fingers. In the end, we had to have her ring specially made because we couldn't find one to fit. If there isn't enough gold in it, the goldsmith says he can add extra metal. But that's OK. The foundation of the new ring will still be Margaret's and that's what matters."

Lucy's throat had gone so dry she couldn't even cough to clear it. She certainly couldn't speak.

"You've got the ring in your safe with the rest of your mother's jewellery, haven't you?" He paused, smiling across at Lucy. "Can you get it out for me, please, love?"

Lucy knew her face must be flaming. She'd heard other people talking about wanting the earth to open and swallow them up. She now knew exactly how they felt. For a second, she was tempted to lie, or at least to put him off until she could work up the courage to tell him the truth.

"Lucy?" He was frowning slightly and sounding uncertain. Not his usual self at all.

Lucy took a deep breath, stood very straight and launched into the confession she'd been avoiding for so many years. "I'm terribly sorry, Dad, but I don't have it. I lost it."

His face blanched into an empty mask. "What do you mean *you lost it*? How could you come to lose it? And why did you take it in the first place? It wasn't yours to take."

"No, it wasn't," she agreed. She swallowed hard. "I was trying to show off to the girls at school. I was the newbie and they'd been making my life a misery and… Well, it doesn't matter what my reasons were. Taking the ring was wrong. And losing it was even worse. It was too small for my ring finger so I wore it on my pinkie.

And it fell off. Somewhere. I've searched and searched but... It's gone for good. I'm so sorry."

"And you never thought to tell me what you'd done?" His voice was hard. And he was ignoring her apology.

"It happened the second Christmas after Mum died and you...you still weren't yourself." Her father had gone even whiter at the mention of his continuing grief. "I kept hoping the ring would turn up. That someone would find it. By the time I finally accepted that it was gone for good, you seemed to be back on an even keel and I didn't want to hurt you all over again. So I didn't say anything."

He raised his eyebrows at her. Normally his eyes were full of warmth when he looked at Lucy. Now they were cold.

Full confession time. It had to be now. No more excuses. "No, that's not the whole truth. The truth is that I was scared to confess what I'd done and so I kept putting it off. And the longer I put it off, the more difficult it was to find a way of telling you. In the end, I shoved it to the back of my mind and tried to forget about it. I'm a coward, Dad. And I'm really sorry. I should have told you years ago."

"Yes, you should," he snapped. He turned his back and stomped out of Lucy's office without another word.

She stood there, frozen, gazing at the empty space and the open office door. She ought to go after him. Apologise again. She—

The front door slammed. She heard his car start up and roar off.

Too late. She gulped and ran a shaky hand through her hair.

He would probably go to the cemetery to put fresh flowers on her mother's grave. And he might talk to the headstone, too. He did that, sometimes. He'd be telling his dead wife what a disappointment their only child had turned out to be. Not only a thief, but a coward as well.

Lucy could feel tears welling up. But she had no right to feel sorry for herself. It was all her own fault. She grabbed her coat and made for the door. She couldn't possibly follow her father. So she'd go for a long walk, across the fields and up into the hills where no one would see her. She would walk until she was too exhausted to think.

She hoped the heavens would open and she'd get soaked. It would serve her right if she caught pneumonia.

It was very late when Lucy got back, chilled to the bone and almost asleep on her feet, but nowhere near a solution to her problems. Her father's car was still missing from its usual place. Most of the Manor was dark when she let herself in. She made a half-hearted circuit of her father's favourite rooms, in case he was there, somewhere, sitting in the dark and brooding.

She knew perfectly well he wasn't one to brood. He was a man of action. That was why he'd decided to turn his love into an enduring symbol that he could wear on his hand. And Lucy had been the one to tear the heart out of his dream.

She dragged her feet to the kitchen and sat down at the long oak table. She hadn't eaten all day, she realised. She supposed she ought to have something. First, she fetched a bottle of wine from the rack and poured herself a large glass. It wouldn't make her thought processes any clearer, she knew, but she needed help to turn off her tumbling brain so that she could eventually get to sleep.

Staring into the middle distance, she sipped. It was

rich and mellow and warming. Exactly what she needed.

When the first glass was empty, she poured another, but she had enough sense to make a slice of toast and scramble a couple of eggs. She even ate most of it, while she downed more of the good red wine. By the time she'd finished her makeshift meal and stacked the dishwasher with her meagre haul of dirty crocks, it was very late. Clearly her father did not plan to return. He'd probably found a hotel for the night. Better than coming home to see the daughter who had betrayed him.

She sighed and made for the stairs and her bed.

At some stage they would face each other and she would apologise. Again. And maybe, in the end, he would forgive her.


Having spent nearly an hour nursing a pint in the pub, Gabe was no longer in a forgiving mood. He checked his mobile for the umpteenth time—no texts, no missed calls. She hadn't bothered to tell him she wouldn't be turning up. And she'd even switched off her mobile so he couldn't reach her to ask why.

Perhaps something had happened to her? Perhaps she wasn't *that* bad-mannered?

Not for the first time, he considered leaving a message on the main phone at the Manor. But what would he say? And what if her PA—or worse, her father—picked up the message?

Nope. Not a good idea. If she'd switched off her mobile, it was because she didn't want to be reached. And specifically not by Gabe.

He could take a hint. She'd probably thought of something better to do than spending time with a dirty-fingered minion like him. Nothing new there.

He swallowed the last of his beer and made for the

door, grunting a barely audible "goodnight" to the landlord and the handful of villagers propping up the bar.

The following morning, Lucy woke late. And cursing. She'd forgotten to set her alarm. And she needed to be on duty for the start of the hunt.

No time to shower or shampoo her hair. She only had time for a quick wash—*a lick and a promise*, her mother had called that, with an understanding smile for the daughter who was so often at risk of being late for school, always as a result of reading far too late into the night.

*What made me remember that?* Lucy thought distractedly. But she didn't have time to work out why her mother was suddenly so much in her thoughts.

She threw on her clothes, dragged a comb through her hair and dashed down to the kitchen. Luckily, the extra staff had already arrived and were laying out the trays for the stirrup cup—port for the grown-ups and fruit juice for the younger riders. The Manor House kept up the old hunting traditions whenever possible. With so many riders for the drag-hunt, though, they were having to use ordinary glasses rather than the traditional silver stirrup cups that riders had to drain and upend.

"Morning, Lucy. Isn't it a lovely day?" Anne said, cheerfully. She lived in the village next to Jane and always helped out when the Manor was busy. "Don't worry, love. Everything's under control."

So even Anne could see at a glance that Lucy wasn't her normal, organised self. Great. Just what she needed.

Anne's husband, Tom, another of the village helpers, appeared at the back door then. "Most of the riders have arrived. Shall we take out the trays, Lucy?"

"Um. How many are there, Tom?" She was expecting

about thirty, but sometimes people turned up on spec when the weather was fine.

"I counted thirty-seven but I think there are more coming down the drive. Lots of youngsters, too. Looks like the Pony Club's put out a three-line whip." He grinned. "You might need an extra tray of the non-alcoholic stuff. Otherwise the little tykes'll be into the port. And then we'd really be in trouble."

Anne nodded and bustled about, preparing another tray of juice.

Lucy picked up a tray of port glasses and made her way down the hall to the front door. There were horses and ponies everywhere, almost too many to count. And the sun was shining low in the cloudless winter sky, catching brasses and polished boots. Lucy carefully threaded her way through to a red-coated rider on a raking bay hunter. She offered her tray. "Morning, Master. Lovely day for it."

The Master of Fox Hounds touched his whip to his hat and reached for a glass. "Thanks, Lucy. Yes, should be a good run," he agreed. He drained his glass in a single swallow and replaced it on Lucy's tray, upside down. "We'll need to be off in about five minutes so any late-comers will just have to catch up." He waved his whip in the direction of the long drive to the Manor gates. Quite a few riders were still arriving, but without any appearance of haste. "The drag set off over a quarter of an hour ago, so we can't leave it much longer. He's promised to lay a broken trail today so that the hounds will have to work a lot harder to pick up the scent. Our last two outings were much too easy." He made a face. "And much too quick, for my taste."

Lucy smiled up into his weather-beaten face. He'd been MFH for as long as she could remember. She knew he would prefer "proper" fox-hunting, but the law was the law, so it had to be drag-hunting these days. "Let's hope your drag foxes you all, good and proper," she quipped.

He groaned. "Was that supposed to be a joke, Lucy? Get along with you."

Lucy winked at him and passed on to offer her tray to the other adult riders. With the rest of her temporary staff offering trays as well, everyone was soon served and the Master was able to set off without delay.

Lucy breathed a sigh of relief. At least one thing had gone well today. Now she could take an hour or so for herself. Her muscles were still protesting as a result of the previous day's hours of scrambling and climbing in the hills, so she decided she would have a long scented bath. And then she'd take special care with doing her hair and make-up. She wanted to look—and smell—her best when her father eventually came back.

# Chapter Fourteen

GABE HEARD THEM LONG before he saw them.

He leapt up from the tree stump where he'd been sitting with his flask of coffee and sprinted out to the edge of the plantation to get a better view. What he saw was a terrified red streak, racing the length of the plantation in search of cover. And then he saw what the poor animal was trying to escape—the hound pack in full cry. The whippers-in were trying to regain control, but failing. With the scent of an escaping fox in their nostrils, the hounds were not for turning.

Behind the hounds, the hunt itself thundered into view. With the Master at the front, of course—Gabe was sure the man would be secretly delighted that his pack had picked up the scent of a real live fox—and what looked like dozens and dozens of galloping riders in his wake.

Gabe tried yelling and waving his arms in an attempt to keep them off his delicate trees, but they paid no attention. The Master's eyes were glued to the fox and the hound pack; the other riders' eyes were fixed on the Master's red coat.

Gabe's growing disbelief soon turned into boiling anger as hundreds of hooves churned up his plantation and trampled his trees into the mud. Within minutes, the whole destructive herd had galloped off into the distance, leaving hundreds of saplings broken, twisted and lost. All those months of backbreaking work, and for what? So that Lucy Cairns's Hooray Henrys could rampage across the countryside, mangling everything at will? Well, Gabe wasn't having any of that.

He wasn't going to have them tearing that poor panic-stricken fox to pieces, either.

The hunt was on unfamiliar private land—Gabe's land—and the fox had been running north in its attempt to escape. But Gabe knew every inch of his terrain and he was pretty sure he could guess where the animal would eventually go to ground, in an earth he'd spotted much further west. What's more, Gabe knew how to get there before the hunt did.

With a quick prayer that the fox would circle round to comparative safety, Gabe raced across to his old pickup and roared off down the lane.

He made it. By a hair. He arrived at the spot in time to see the fox's brush disappearing into its earth, deep in an impenetrable tangle of bramble and woody undergrowth. He steered his old pickup through the trees and heavy ground cover and parked it across the only entrance to the thicket. Then, with a grim smile, he got out and climbed on to the bonnet. He was determined to get the better of the hunt. *The whip hand*, he decided. He wasn't planning to lose in this encounter.

He didn't have to wait long. He was soon surrounded by belling hounds, desperate to get to the fox, but

154

impeded by the dense vegetation. And by Gabe's vehicle.

The riders in the wake of the hounds had to push their way through, too, which slowed them down a lot. The Master, still in the front, was yelling orders to his huntsmen, but stopped in mid-sentence when he saw Gabe, staring down at him from the bonnet with his arms folded across his chest. Gabe thought he might have caught the word "terriers" but he couldn't be sure. It wouldn't have surprised him, though.

"That's far enough," Gabe shouted, spreading his arms wide. "This is private land. Your quarry has gone to ground and it's against the law for you to dig it out. If you try, I'll make sure my photographs of your illegal hunt are sent to the police. *And* all the tabloids." Gabe didn't have his mobile with him, so he had nothing to take photos with, but he was prepared to lay odds that the hunt wouldn't dare to call his bluff. Not when they'd been caught red-handed. "Now, get off my land."

The Master, who'd gone very red in the face, swallowed hard, as if he were about to argue. But after a minute, he called to the whippers-in to get the hounds under control. He knew he'd lost. He made to turn his horse and retreat the way he'd come.

"No," Gabe shouted. "You've already done enough damage to my land. There's a lane over there." He pointed. "You leave by the public road. All of you. Dogs as well. And keep those blighters away from the earth."

The Master didn't apologise. But he did nod. And then he motioned to the riders to follow him out to the lane. It took longer to get the hounds under control but eventually they were gone, too. Gabe didn't move until he was sure there was no longer any danger to the fox. He jumped down and crossed to the brambles. "You're OK for today, old fellow," he said in the direction of the earth, "but, if I were you, I'd stay underground when the hunt's about."

Once he was sure it was safe to leave, he drove back to the plantation to assess the damage. It turned out to be much worse than he'd thought and his fury reignited. The plantation would have to be completely renewed and replanted. He swore aloud. All that work, wasted.

Well, he was not going to break his own back doing the work all over again. Next stop, the Manor House. Lucy, and her father, would have to agree to pay. Gabe was planning to lay the bill squarely at Lucy's feet. And she was going to get an earful from him while he did it.

A woman who broke her word deserved everything she got.

Lucy was coming down the stairs as he walked through the kitchen and into the hall in search of her. She looked—and smelled—divine, which did nothing at all for Gabe's seething temper. Had she spent last night in some fancy spa somewhere, instead of meeting Gabe in the pub as she'd promised?

What she said was not divine. "Do you have to walk your mud all through the house, Gabe?" She pointed at his filthy boots. "You might have taken those off by the door."

That was the absolute end. Gabe exploded. "What I've done to your floor is nothing compared to what your damned horses have done to my plantation."

"What are you talking about?"

"Your blasted hunt, Lucy Cairns. It chased a fox through my plantation and turned the whole place into something that looks like the Somme. Except that today's casualties are my trees. The fox escaped, but I doubt there's a single one of my trees that hasn't been uprooted, or broken, or bent. They'll all have to be dug out and

156

replaced. And it needs to be done by the end of January if I'm to recoup anything from this disaster. That's down to you, Lucy Cairns. Hire some men. Get some new whips. And get them all planted. Otherwise I'm going to sue you for all the damage your poncey mates have done today."

Lucy had gone pale under her artful make-up. She was clutching at the banister. "But the hunt shouldn't have gone anywhere near the plantation. Oh God!" A visible tremor ran through her. "The extra marshals. I forgot."

"So that's why the whippers-in couldn't control the hounds. *You* didn't do your job. I might have known. Call yourself a businesswoman? You're useless. Incompetent. You're a walking disaster, Lucy Cairns. And an apology for a—"

"That's quite enough from you, Bliss!" Sir Drew's voice cut in from the end of the hall. He marched forward to glare at Gabe. "Who the hell do you think you are to come into my house and speak to my daughter like that? I'll thank you to leave. Now!"

When Gabe opened his mouth to protest, Sir Drew yelled, "No, not another word! Get out of my house! And tomorrow, I'm going to see my solicitor about ending your lease. No matter what it costs me."

Gabe drew himself up and looked down his nose at the older man. "Aye, money talks," he spat. "As ever." And before Sir Drew could say another word, Gabe turned on his heel and stalked out.

"Dad, I—"

"Whatever you have to say, I don't want to hear it. You'll want to defend him, I suppose. Don't. There's no defence for behaviour like that. And tomorrow, I'm going to break his lease. I'll show him that no one crosses Drew Cairns. If Bliss wants his precious tree nursery, he can find it somewhere else." He marched out, following in Gabe's footsteps.

Lucy collapsed in a heap on the bottom stair and dropped her head into her hands. There was nothing to choose between them. Both furious, both stubborn, both totally convinced they were right. They wanted to tear each other limb from limb. Neither would be happy until there was blood on the floor.

It was all Lucy's fault, but she hadn't a clue how to prevent the disaster that was coming. Gabe would lose his livelihood. And his dream. He would hate Lucy—if he didn't already—for causing the failure of his business. Sir Drew had already decided that his only child had betrayed him and wasn't to be trusted any more. And he was going to take his anger out on Gabe, by breaking the lease on the nursery.

Lucy knew she'd been a coward over the ring. And she'd been a complete flake over the hunt. She'd failed to organise enough stewards for so many riders. If there had been more of them, would they have been able to stop the hounds going after a real fox rather than the drag? Possibly. Probably. She couldn't be sure, but marshals could at least have tried. As it was, no one had stood between hundreds of galloping hooves and Gabe's beloved plantation.

The damage was her fault. It would cost thousands to put it right.

And arranging stewards wasn't the only thing that had gone completely out of her mind, she realised, shocked. She'd stood Gabe up, too!

"I'll be there," she'd said.

And then forgotten all about her promise because, after that horrible moment of confession to her father, she'd been feeling too sorry for herself to think straight.

She'd failed her father and she'd failed Gabe. He had put months of back-breaking work into that plantation and Lucy's incompetence had allowed the hunt to ruin it in minutes. No wonder Gabe was attacking her for indulging her over-paid, over-pampered, over-prettified clients and their self-entitled ways. Lucy herself was probably no better in his eyes.

And what could she do to put things right? How could she appeal to her father when he clearly couldn't bear to listen to a word she said? He'd refused to let her explain what had happened. And in his present temper, he certainly wouldn't allow her to plead Gabe's case. Not after the insults he'd heard Gabe hurling at Lucy. It didn't matter that Gabe was truly the injured party here. Sir Drew had decided that it would be right and proper to throw Gabe off his land. Would he really do it? Was there any way to change his mind?

Lucy decided that, if she had to go down on her knees to persuade her father to listen, she would do it. She'd had enough of being a coward where he was concerned.

Gabe wanted to throw things. Mostly at Lucy.

She'd screwed up everything. His plantation was a sea of mud. And his landlord was going to ruin him. However strong the lease, Sir Drew could find a way to break it. He had the money to pay for the cleverest lawyers. And he was known for being a man of his word. Even if today's word was "eviction".

Gabe forced himself to drive slowly and carefully back to the nursery. He mustn't let his emotions get the better of him. That was a recipe for ending up in a ditch.

His Lucy? Not any more. The Lucy of his dream would never have betrayed him as modern-day Lucy had. The Lucy of his dream was well and truly gone.

What was it she'd said when he told her what those mad devils had done?

Actually, he hadn't let her say anything much at all. The moment she'd admitted to having forgotten to organise the marshals, he'd started shouting abuse at her.

She'd clearly been upset about what the hunt had done. And about her part in it. She'd stood there, clutching the banister, and shaking. He would never get that image out of his mind.

Gabe was ashamed of the way he'd behaved to her. He'd let his anger overcome his manners. But it was too late now to go back and apologise. Sir Drew would probably never let Gabe cross the threshold again. Besides, the damage was done—to the plantation, to Gabe's relationship with Lucy, to his future. He'd lose all the savings that he'd invested in the nursery. He'd have nowhere to live, either. So he'd probably have to go back to being a jobbing gardener, working for the kind of employer he detested—a jumped-up know-it-all toff with more money than sense.

Great. Just great.

Lucy's father didn't come back to the Manor that night either. Why did men have to be so stubborn? She couldn't help remembering a line from a poem she'd learned at school: "nursing his wrath to keep it warm." Was that what her father was doing? And Gabe, too?

If she couldn't talk to them, she couldn't begin to make them see sense. Actually, she would have liked to knock their heads together. Unfortunately, head-knocking was off limits to a girl who was so deeply in the wrong with both her men.

Her father appeared at lunch time the following day.

His colour was much more normal, Lucy was glad to see. And he wasn't looking at her with the distant coldness that had frightened her so much.

"Well, I talked to old Barrett. The nursery lease will take a lot of breaking. And it's going to cost me a packet." Sir Drew shook his head. "Barrett's advice is not to do it, of course, but he's a lawyer. He would say that. I'm damned if I will go along with him, though." His voice was beginning to rise in anger. "Not after what that low-life said to you yesterday. I'm going to—"

"Dad, don't do it. Please." She risked putting her hand on his arm.

He shrugged her off. "What? After the way he treated you? You're suggesting I should listen to him insulting my daughter and let him stay on my land?"

"Everything he said was justified." She took both her father's hands and forced him to look her in the eye. Then she repeated what she'd said, word for word. "Everything he said was justified."

Sir Drew's eyes widened. "What?"

"The hunt trampled his plantation. Months of work destroyed in minutes."

"But—"

"It was my fault, Dad. After you and I— Well, never mind that. What matters is that I forgot to arrange the extra marshals for the hunt. It was my responsibility and I failed. So when the hounds caught the scent of a real fox, there weren't enough men to turn them. And of course the horses all followed the hounds. It was my fault, Dad," she said again.

"So you want me to change my mind?" His neck was turning red. "You want me to apologise to Bliss?"

She shook her head. The fault was not his. "No. That's for me to do. All I'm asking you to do, Dad—and if you

161

want me to plead, I will—is not to break Gabe's lease. He doesn't deserve that. Not after all the work he's put in at the nursery. Everything that happened was my fault, not his. I admit he lost his temper a bit yesterday, and called me a few names, but in his place you'd probably have done the same. I deserved it."

"Hmm."

"Please, Dad."

"I'll...I'll think about it. I'm not promising, mind, but I'll give Barrett a call and tell him to put things on hold for a few days."

She wanted to hug him but it wasn't the right moment for that. They had to get back to their old easy rapport first. So Lucy thanked her father for listening to what she had to say and went off to the farm shop in hopes of putting things right with Gabe.

She found him in the car park outside the shop. "I owe you an apology, Gabe."

"Just the one?"

Lucy bristled. She couldn't help herself. "Isn't one enough?"

"Actually, no. Think about it. You let your idiot hunt devastate my plantation. You let your father believe I was insulting you without good reason. And you even stood me up in the pub two nights ago. What more could a man want? I don't think we have anything to say to each other, Miss Cairns. Do you?" He turned away.

Before he could stomp off, Lucy grabbed his sleeve. "Now, look here, Gabriel Bliss. It's time you and I got a few things straight. Yes, I stood you up the other night, but I didn't mean to. I'd had a...a quarrel with my father. I was really upset. I clean forgot about our arrangement. OK?"

"Same as you *forgot* to ensure that the hunt would be nowhere near the nursery?"

"Pretty much. I told you. I was upset. I went for a long walk in the hills. Everything else went out of my mind. I'm sorry, OK? I'm really sorry. I know how much work you've put into the plantation."

"Well, it doesn't matter now, since I won't have it for much longer. Your father's breaking the lease. You've won on all counts, Lucy Cairns."

"No, I haven't. And you won't lose the lease if I can help it. Dad was furious. *He* can call me names, but no one else can. So he took his anger out on you. I don't think he means to go through with his threat."

"You don't think? Aye, that's the truth. You don't *think*."

Lucy gasped at the insult. Then she swore at him and made to slap his face.

But he was too quick for her. He caught her wrist and held it firm. "Oh, no, you don't."

She wanted to scream at him. And she wanted to weep in her frustration. How had it all gone so wrong? How come they were hating each other? And her dad, too?

And then Gabe did the most extraordinary thing. With his free hand he carefully brushed away the single hot tear that had escaped down her cheek. "It's not worth your tears, Lucy. It's only a piece of land." He caressed her face, ever so gently. "I'll find somewhere new. Forget it. Forget it all." With that, he turned and walked calmly into the shop.

Lucy was so astonished she could neither speak nor move. By the time she regained enough control to react, Gabe was gone.

163

## Chapter Fifteen

GABE WAS SITTING IN his flat above the shop, brooding over a cup of coffee. At some stage, he'd have to go back to the plantation to retrieve his abandoned flask. At the moment, though, it was much more important to try to sort out what was going on in the tangled spaghetti of his mind.

His mobile pinged. A text. From Lucy. He groaned. That was the last thing he needed.

*IOU apols 2 & 3. Feathers at 7? OK?*

He hadn't expected that from her. It was clearly an olive branch. And a generous one. If he turned her down, she might never give him another chance. So, before his brain could remind him of all the good reasons for refusing, he texted back: *OK*.

Too late, he realised the downsides of what he'd just agreed to. Why on earth had he gone along with meeting her in such a public place? With Gabe's luck, half the village would be in *The Feathers* this time, watching them avidly.

164

Great. Just great.

And what on earth was he going to say to her when they were face to face? That stupid gesture when he'd brushed away her tears. How could he explain that? And what he'd said to her, too?

He probably wouldn't have to explain; she probably wouldn't ask. But it would hang here between them. And it was too late to change his mind about the meeting; it would be cowardly to back out now.

Why had he touched her anyway? Why had he stroked her cheek?

Because she was upset. Because his response to her attempted apology had been crass and downright nasty. Because he was ashamed of his bullying behaviour.

Because he loved her?

*Don't go there, Gabe. She's the boss's daughter.*

Unfortunately, once the thought had been voiced, even to himself, he couldn't put it out of his mind. Victorian Gabe had loved Victorian Lucy. He could admit that. It was a love-match across the divide—a divide much wider and deeper than the one that separated him from modern-day Lucy—but it had been made to work. Why couldn't the modern relationship work, too?

Gabe's conscience reminded him that the distancing had been all his doing. He was the one who insisted on calling her "Miss Cairns" and stressing the gulf between them. She had asked for them to be friends. She wanted them to be "Gabe" and "Lucy".

And she was the one who had saved him after the concussion. She was the one who had looked after him. He should at least be grateful, instead of biting her nose off. A little less stubborn pride and a little more give-and-take were called for, he told himself, in a moment of

165

mortifying self-awareness. When he met her in the pub, he would have to be a model of good manners and reasonableness.

He could to keep that up for half and hour, couldn't he?

Well, yes. Probably.

Provided there was no touching.

Gabe dressed carefully for his visit to *The Feathers*—a clean shirt and his best sweater, the one with no moth holes. It was a business meeting, after all, and he owed it to Lucy to appear respectable. Not too respectable, though, or the village would be gossiping even more about Gabe Bliss and the millionaire's daughter.

It wasn't raining, but there was a bitingly cold wind. He pulled on his padded jacket, stuffing his high-vis gloves into the pockets. He might need those on the walk back. Since the pub served excellent craft beer, he would leave his pickup at home this time and enjoy their hospitality. Whatever Lucy did.

*The Feathers* was warm and welcoming. Unfortunately for Gabe, it was also heaving with customers. It turned out that Lucy had picked the night when the local league played its darts match. Their meeting would have loads of spectators—not only the whole village but probably half the county as well.

"Evenin', Gabe." Tom grinned at Gabe. "Come to support the team, have you?" Tom was the best darts player in the village. If he was on form, the opposition wouldn't stand a chance.

Gabe smiled back. "Course. Got to show solidarity. But I need a beer first." He shouldered his way to the bar and ordered, watching as Joe, the landlord, drew his pint slowly and carefully. *The Feathers* prided itself on how it served fine beers and the landlord wouldn't allow the process to be rushed, even when the pub was busy.

Gabe spotted a vacant table in the far corner, well away from the dart board, and pushed his way through to it. With luck, the other customers would be so engrossed in the match they wouldn't pay too much attention to Gabe and his companion. When—if?—Lucy arrived.

She was there before he realised. Standing at the other side of the table, smiling down at him. "I'm not late, am I, Gabe?"

He closed his mouth, gulped, and tried to smile back. Then he remembered his promised good manners and leapt to his feet, gesturing to her to take his vacant place. "No, of course not. Er– what can I get you, Lucy?"

Her eyes widened. "White wine, please. And it's nice that you're calling me 'Lucy' at last. I'm glad that bang on the head knocked some sense into you, Gabe."

What could he possibly do now? He'd said it because he'd been unable to get Victorian Lucy out of his thoughts. So now he'd have to stick with it. "You've been so kind since the accident. A regular trooper. So, since it's what you want, I thought I should go along with it." It sounded lame. And it wasn't true, either. "It would be churlish not to agree," he added. Good grief, he sounded like his Victorian *alter ego*. "I mean," he stammered, "it would be childish to keep objecting."

Her eyes were laughing up at him.

"I'll get your drink," he mumbled and fled to the bar.

"Chardonnay, sauvignon blanc or pinot grigio? Large glass or small?" Joe asked.

Gabe hadn't a clue. And, just at the moment, he needed a bit of distance from Lucy so he wasn't prepared to go back and ask, or to yell a question across the crowded pub with everyone listening. Mentally crossing his fingers, he said, "Small. Pinot grigio, please," and dug into his pocket for his wallet. If he'd made the right choice, it would be a good omen. If not? Well, this meeting was probably doomed anyway.

He managed not to spill any of the wine as he forced his way back to her through the noisy but good-humoured crowd. He set the glass down carefully. "Pinot grigio," he said, sitting down.

"Fine," she replied evenly.

*That could mean anything*, Gabe thought. Probably not a good start. He took a deep breath and launched into his prepared speech. "I wanted to talk to you about your Christmas tree, without involving your father. You'll be wanting the tree, whatever happens about the lease, and—"

"I told you, Gabe. I'm sure—well, almost sure—that your lease is safe. And don't you want to hear my apologies? You did say you were owed three and you've only had the one, so far."

Definitely an olive branch. Gabe felt some of his tensions leaving him. He sipped at his beer and smiled across at her. "Shall we take those as read? And I need to apologise, too. I said things I'm ashamed of, both at the Manor and later, at the shop. Perhaps we can forget it all? On both sides?"

"Well…" She picked up her wine and took a long swig, almost emptying the little glass. "Your plantation is still ruined, Gabe. What about that?"

That was serious stuff. And he didn't really want to go there. "Can we park that for the moment, Lucy? It depends on what your father does about the lease, in any case. If I lose the nursery, it'll be someone else's problem, won't it?" He wasn't sure he'd managed to keep the bitterness out of his voice.

Lucy reached out to touch his hand in sympathy.

Gabe flinched. He couldn't help himself.

Lucy reared back. Then she tossed off the rest of her wine and stood up. "My round, I think." She gestured to his almost-full glass. "Another pint? Which beer is it?"

Gabe shook his head. "Later," he muttered.

Lucy nodded and left him without another word.

Inwardly, she was seething. What was it with Gabe Bliss? He was clearly hurting but the last thing he'd accept was sympathy from her.

"Another glass of wine, Lucy?" Joe asked genially.

"Yes. Actually, no. I think I'll have a whisky and ginger. Just cooking whisky, please. No ice."

"Single or double?"

"Double." She needed some Dutch courage for this awkward meeting with Gabe. Wine didn't cut it. Scotch might help her strained nerves, too.

But she upended the little can of ginger into the glass before she took it back to the table. She didn't want to advertise that she was drinking doubles. "So," she said amiably, sitting down again, "you were saying? About my tree?"

"Um, yes. There's only one in the whole arboretum that's big enough for what you want. In fact, it's much taller than you need but, as we discussed before, it can be cut to size. It's a beautiful tree. You'll like it, I think. If you can come to the arboretum, I'll show it to you and then we can decide about when to fell it."

Lucy suspected he didn't want to fell it at all. It sounded as though it might be one of the oldest specimens in the collection. But she might be wrong about that. She couldn't decide until she'd seen it for herself. And seen Gabe's reaction to it. "I can come tomorrow, if you like. In the morning?"

169

"I'm around all day," he said. "What say we meet at the shop around ten?" He took a long slug of his beer, avoiding Lucy's eye.

"Fine," she agreed.

In the awkward silence that followed, they both drank again. And again. Lucy reckoned Gabe was trying as hard as she was to think of a topic of conversation. Unfortunately, they were both failing. In the end, she pointed at his half-empty glass. "Ready for another pint now? It's still my round."

"Just a half, thanks. It's Wobbles Gold."

"Great name for a beer." She crossed to the bar to order. "A half of Wobbles, please, Joe. And another double scotch and ginger for me." Joe gave her a sideways look but said nothing while he poured the drinks and took her cash.

At that moment, a great cheer went up from around the dart board. The local team had won a crucial set. "Shall we go over and provide some extra support?" Lucy suggested when she'd taken their drinks back to the table. If the two of them were supporting the village team, they wouldn't have to make conversation with each other.

Gabe agreed immediately. So he'd been feeling embarrassed, too. He emptied the new half-pint of beer into his original glass and followed Lucy to join the crowd around the dart board. Lucy had a couple more drinks while they cheered on the team. Gabe had another two half-pints. Eventually, the village won.

Lucy gave Tom a congratulatory hug. He was the star of the team, after all. At his side, Anne was grinning. She was the captain of the ladies' team and a terrific darts player in her own right. "Time to get another round in for the visiting team," Tom said. "Another drink for you, Lucy?"

She shook her head. She realised she was feeling a little bit light-headed. "No. But thanks for the offer, Tom. I think it's time I made tracks."

Lucy dug into her pocket for her car keys.

"No, you don't." Gabe reached across and plucked the keys out of her fingers. "You're in no fit state to drive anywhere after the amount you've put away." He gestured towards her empty whisky glass.

How many whiskies had she actually had? He knew he was right that she wasn't fit to drive. "Then I'll walk home," she retorted sniffily. "It's not far."

"It's over a mile. And it's dark."

She dug into her pocket again and produced her mobile phone. After quite a lot of fiddling—Gabe could see that she was all fingers and thumbs—she found the torch function and shone it directly into Gabe's eyes. "There you go. It's called a torch. It allows you to see in the dark."

Smiling indulgently, he took the phone out of her hand to check the state of the battery. "You really think this is going to shine all the way back to the Manor House? Phone batteries are notoriously unreliable. What if it runs out halfway?"

"If I can't see my way, I'll find somewhere to shelter until it gets light," she protested.

Gabe felt vindicated. She was slurring her words, though only a little.

"You'll die of hypothermia, you mean." He wanted to shake some sense into her, but she wasn't going to see any kind of sense until she sobered up. Quite a lot. He sighed and pushed himself away from the wall he'd been leaning on. He hadn't drunk nearly as much as Lucy, but he was definitely over the limit. So he couldn't offer to drive her Land Rover. "You can't walk home by yourself. I'll come with you."

"No! You can't—"

"You don't have to talk to me. You don't even have to walk beside me if you can't bear my company. But I'll be right behind you. Every step of the way. That's not negotiable, so you might as well accept it. Now go and get your things. It's cold out there so you need to wrap up."

He said his farewells to Joe and the darts players, congratulating them again. Then he followed Lucy into the hallway to collect his jacket. His gloves were no longer in his pockets. Lucy Cairns was wearing them. The cheek of her!

"You half-inched my gloves, you thieving hussy!" He grinned, pointing accusingly at her hands. She was wearing a high-vis vest as well. Where had she nicked that from?

"So what if I did?" Lucy retorted. "You told me to wrap up and I don't have any of my own. I'll return them. Eventually." She smiled smugly. "I half-inched Tom's high-vis vest, as well. Safer for walking along an unlit road."

"There's a law against that, you know."

"Is there? Going to arrest me then, are you?"

"Someone probably should. But I don't think it will be me. You'd sling me off my land if I did that."

"No, I wouldn't. I w–wouldn't dare. You belong here, Gabriel Bliss." She took a couple of wobbly steps towards the door. "You and the land and the trees. You belong together."

"Hmm." He opened the door for her. They went out into the night together and started along the road. She was definitely not walking in a straight line. "You said you could walk home, Lucy. That might be safe enough. But it certainly isn't safe to *sway* home, the way you're doing. Come on, my girl. Let me keep you on the straight and narrow." He put an arm round her waist and pulled her into his side so that they would have to walk in step and he could ensure she stayed upright.

"You're only doing that 'cause you don't have any gloves," she said, with the irrefutable logic that whisky had provided.

"If you say so," he responded, hugging her closer. "Come on. Let's get you home before something else happens."

Lucy couldn't quite remember how they reached her door. But she had been relishing the feel of Gabe's arm around her and the warmth of his body against hers. It felt right. And safe. She didn't want it to end.

Unfortunately, it did. As soon as they arrived at the back door to the Manor, he let her go. The porch light was shining down on Lucy but Gabe stepped back from its friendly glow. "I'll leave you here, Lucy. You'll be OK inside, won't you?"

"But it's cold out here. Come in. I c–can make c–coffee."

Gabe shook his head at her. He was smiling—a little—but it was clear he'd made up his mind. Even in Lucy's slightly woozy state, she could tell he was back in stubborn mode.

"Your father warned me off, remember? So thanks, but no. I won't be coming in until Sir Drew invites me."

Men! And male pride! There was no way to deal with it.

Actually, Lucy realised, there was.

Before he could make a move to leave, she closed the distance between them, slid her arms round his neck and started to kiss him. When he tried to resist, she tightened her hold and deepened the kiss. Quite soon, he stopped actively resisting. Eventually, he began to kiss her back as she'd known he would. He wanted her; she wanted him. Kissing was the most obvious first step for both of them.

And it was wonderful. She wanted it to go on and on.

It didn't. It couldn't.

"No," Gabe finally groaned against her mouth. He used his superior strength to unwind her arms and push her back against the door so there was space between their bodies. And so that he didn't have to support her. "We can't do this, Lucy. You've had far too much to drink to know what you're doing—"

"No, I—"

"—and you'll regret it in the morning. Give me the jacket and I'll be off."

"What?" She had no idea what he was talking about.

"Tom's high-vis jacket. You *borrowed* it, remember? If I take it back to the pub now, there's a chance he won't have missed it."

He might as well have chucked a bucket of water over her.

She struggled to take off the jacket. In the end, Gabe had to help her. He didn't touch anything but her clothing in the process, though. Clever Gabe. Clever, stubborn Gabe.

"You can return my gloves some other time," he added, turning to go.

She wanted to pull off his gloves and throw them at him, but her coordination wasn't up to such grand gestures. The night had almost swallowed him by the

174

time she'd got the first one off. "Damn you, Gabe," she yelled, frustrated.

His wicked laugh sang back to her from the darkness. "Tomorrow will be fine. Ten o'clock at the farm shop. You won't forget this time, will you, Lucy?"

# Chapter Sixteen

"NO MORE ALCOHOL," LUCY groaned at her reflection in the bathroom mirror. "Not ever."

She looked utterly dreadful—blotchy skin and bleary eyes. Her head was pounding, too. And no wonder. How much whisky had she drunk in the pub? At least three doubles, maybe more. There was Dutch courage and then again, there was sheer idiocy. She should have known better. She *did* know better. She was normally very measured about how much she drank.

But Gabriel Bliss seemed to turn all her self-imposed rules upside down.

She was going to have to face Gabe again, too. This time, she hadn't forgotten. She was due to meet him at ten in order to view her special Christmas tree. One look at her and he would be bound to realise she had a dreadful hangover. She didn't imagine he would sympathise. Why should he? He might even laugh.

No, Gabe wouldn't laugh at her self-inflicted misfortunes. He wasn't that kind of guy. She had to admit that he'd been kind and considerate at the end of their "date" last night. He'd insisted on walking her home and seeing her safely to her door. And he had very politely—and very gently—turned down her sexual advances.

Lucy looked in the mirror again. Now she was bright red at the very thought of what she had done on the doorstep. She might as well have stripped off her clothes and danced a drunken jig for him. She groaned again. In mortification, this time.

She wasn't enough of a coward to duck out of this morning's meeting, though. She was going to have to apologise to Gabe. *Again.*

Dressed, and with makeup concealing the worst of the previous night's ravages, Lucy sat hunched over her second mug of strong black coffee, trying to work out exactly what she was going to say to Gabe. She checked her watch. Quarter past nine, so she had less than half an hour's rehearsal time. She was determined not to be late at the farm shop. Gabe would definitely not have anything to reproach her with.

Except last night's little exhibition on the doorstep, of course.

"Morning, Lucy."

"Oh. Dad. I wasn't— I didn't expect to see you this morning." Her voice was croaky. Would he notice?

He sat down opposite her, reaching for the coffee pot and a spare mug. "Black coffee? That's not like you. Not in the mornings. Out on the town last night, were we?" He twinkled at her as he stirred milk into his coffee.

That sounded so much more like their normal banter that Lucy made a huge effort to respond in kind. "I was in *The Feathers*. It was darts match night. We won, too."

"So that's the reason for the black coffee, eh? Well, I'm glad you were there to support the local team. And talking of support..." He fixed his eyes on his mug and said, slowly, "There's something I need to ask you, Lucy."

That sounded serious. Lucy held her breath and waited.

"When we, um, spoke about your mother's ring, you said— Actually, I didn't take it all in at the time. What was that about having problems at school?"

Lucy gulped. "Well," she began, but no words came.

Her father reached across and put his hand over hers. "How old were you when you lost the ring, Lucy?"

"Oh. Um, I'm not sure. Twelve or thirteen, I think."

"Twelve or thirteen," he repeated. "And you were being bullied at school. And I was so taken up with my own grief that I didn't even notice. A sad excuse for a parent I turned out to be. I'm so very sorry, love. I should have been there for you—you'd lost your mother, for heaven's sake—but I failed you. I was selfish and self-indulgent and—"

"And a wonderful father," she burst out. "You loved me. I knew that. You couldn't bring yourself to talk about Mum. Even to me. I understood that, too."

"So you were looking after me, even though you were only a child. Why didn't I see it at the time? You were the grown-up back then, not me. It's taken me far too many years to realise what a rock you've been for me, love. Then and now." He shook his head sadly. This was a vulnerable side to him that Lucy hadn't seen before. "And about the ring..."

"Dad, I'm really—"

"Forget about it. It was only a piece of metal." He squeezed Lucy's hand. "It's nothing compared to what

I've got with you, Lucy. Margaret's daughter. And mine."

They sat in silence for several minutes, holding hands. A moment to treasure.

And then Sir Andrew Cairns, hard-headed millionaire businessman, reasserted himself over Lucy's doting dad. He cleared his throat noisily and rose from the table. "I need to be going."

Lucy smiled lovingly at him and nodded. OK, tycoons didn't do soppy handholding. Not as a rule. But this one had. She knew how much it had cost him to make that apology. And how much he loved her.

"Got to visit a new client this morning," he added. "And I've an appointment with Barrett later, too."

"Barrett? About Gabe's lease?"

"Well, yes. I've decided he can stay. Tell him, will you?" he added briskly, making for the door. That was as close as he would ever get to making an apology to an outsider like Gabe. But it was enough.

Hangover almost forgotten, she danced out of the kitchen and across the yard to Maisie.

As she put the key in the ignition, she remembered that she had an apology of her own to make. Her sunny mood clouded a little. Then she squared her shoulders and put Maisie in gear.

Gabe had started work early but he was back at the shop well before ten. Muffin, daft dog, greeted him as though they hadn't seen each other for years. The little fellow wouldn't stop twisting around Gabe's legs until he'd been suitably patted and scratched, either. Chuckling, Gabe gave in at once. Poor old Muffin deserved a little attention in return for all the fun and companionship he provided.

Gabe retrieved his mobile from Jane and switched it

on, too, though there were no messages. He'd been wondering if he might get a text from Lucy, postponing their meeting. She ought to have a monumental hangover, unless she had a much harder head than anyone else he knew. There was also the question of driving. Would she still be over the limit this morning? It was possible. But there was very little chance of her being stopped on the lane from the Manor to the farm shop. At least, he hoped so, for her sake.

She drove up on the dot of ten o'clock, backing Maisie expertly into the marked bay. Impressive, Gabe thought. She must be awash with black coffee to have sobered up so well.

"Morning, Lucy," he called as she swung out of the driving seat. "How're you doing?"

She pulled a face. "As well as can be expected." Her voice was at least half an octave lower than normal. "Thank you *so* much for asking."

"Ah. Er—sorry. Didn't mean to rub it in. But I'm really glad you made it, anyway. It's a lovely morning so you'll see your tree at its best." He started for his pickup. "I'll drive, shall I?"

She made no move to follow him.

He turned back. "What's the matter? Don't you trust my driving?"

"You're going to pretend it didn't happen, aren't you?"

"Er—*it*?" He was pretty sure what *it* meant, but he wasn't going to volunteer anything. He'd had no intention of referring to that sizzling kiss ever again. At least, not unless Lucy herself did. He'd known at the time that it would be wrong to take advantage of her tipsy state, but that didn't mean he hadn't been tempted. Very tempted. Apart from the whisky, she had tasted exactly like Victorian Lucy. And with that Lucy, Gabe had gone much, much further. To the satisfaction of both of them.

He knew exactly what he'd missed out on. Even if this Lucy didn't.

She frowned at him. Then she drew herself up very straight, fixing her gaze on a point beyond Gabe's left shoulder. "I owe you another apology." She sounded like a prisoner pleading guilty in court. "I'm sorry I, er, came on so strong last night. Especially after you'd been kind enough to see me home." She let out a long breath and her shoulders relaxed a bit. Did that signify duty done?

Gabe nodded absently. He was in two minds about how to reply. Part of him was issuing a stern warning: *don't go there; you don't know where it might lead.* Part of him wanted to tell her how much he'd enjoyed it. That he'd very much like to do *it* again on a future occasion, when she hadn't had too much to drink.

He dithered too long, trying to make up his mind what to say.

In the end, Lucy decided for him. She smiled up at him and said, simply, "Thanks, Gabe. You're a trooper. Shall we go and see the tree? One Christmas tree to go?"

Decision made. "Sure." He opened the passenger door for her. "Hop in."


It was an absolute whopper of a tree, seventy or eighty feet high. And with a girth to match.

"We'll have to take off the bottom thirty feet or so, unfortunately, or we'll never even get it through your door." Gabe took a step back and gazed up at the top of the monster tree. "But the top forty feet is a beautiful shape. No one will guess we've had to trim it to size."

Lucy reached out to grasp one of the lower branches and run her hand down it. The needles felt quite soft and pliable, especially at the very end. They'd be newer needles, she supposed, this year's growth. In future years, they'd firm up more, and darken, and new young growth would replace them as the branches spread even further. There would be new cones, too.

"How old is it, do you reckon, Gabe?"

"Um. I honestly don't know. Eighty years maybe? A hundred? Once we've felled it, I'll be able to count the rings and tell you." The blasted man was being determinedly upbeat about it all. Didn't he care that he was about to kill a beautiful old tree, one that should still have decades of life in front of it?

"Give me a minute, Gabe," she said throatily. She wandered round to the far side of the huge tree, where Gabe couldn't see her. She pulled down another branch, from higher up this time, and stroked it against her cheek. This one was a bit more prickly. As if the tree were trying to fight back? As if it were struggling for life?

She couldn't do it. It wasn't the hangover talking; it was her sense of what was right with the world. She'd told Gabe that he and the land and the trees belonged together—she did remember saying that to him—and yet she'd been planning to murder one of the finest specimens he had. And for what? So that her pampered guests could smell and touch a bit of Christmas for a day or so, before it was chucked on the bonfire and burnt to cinders.

She padded quietly back round to the other side, stroking branches as she went. And found Gabe. He had sunk his face into the tree. And his arms were round as many branches as he could reach.

He didn't jump back when he realised she was there. He let go, but slowly, caressing the branches. He looked defiant, and proud of himself, as if he were glad that she'd caught him communing with his tree. And he didn't say a single word. He simply gazed at her, with sadness in his eyes as he waited for her verdict.

"It's a beautiful tree, Gabe. Perfect for the stairwell." She reached out to stroke another branch. "But it looks much more beautiful here. I don't want it cut down."

"Are you absolutely sure, Lucy? We did make a deal. And this is the only tree that fits the bill." He was trying to be businesslike. As her father had, earlier.

Lucy wasn't fooled. Gabe's glowing eyes betrayed him. She forced a laugh, though it sounded brittle in her ears. "Are you worried I'll take my business somewhere else? I promise I won't. You'll get your profit, somehow. But I'm afraid I can't help feeling sentimental about this magnificent tree."

"I think that may make two of us." He closed the distance between them so that their bodies were nearly touching. His voice dropped to a whisper. "I know I turned you down last night, but if the offer is still open, I'd very much like to kiss you."

Now it was Lucy's turn to glow. She slid her arms round his neck and pulled him closer. "You, Gabriel Bliss, are a prize idiot, you know that? I'm hung over, I look like a wreck, and you want to kiss me?"

"I do." He moved even closer. "One other thing, Lucy Cairns."

"Mmm?" She threaded her fingers into his thick hair.

"You talk too much. But I have a cure for that."

His cure worked extremely well. It was a long time before either of them spoke another word.

There was no touching, no handholding, when they got back to the farm shop. Both were too conscious that Jane might see. And draw conclusions. They had reached an

183

unspoken understanding that they didn't want the whole village gossiping about their relationship.

Whatever kind of relationship it was.

In fact, Lucy wasn't at all sure. But she knew—and she was sure Gabe knew, too—that there *was* now a relationship. When a man's kisses had the power to set the ends of your hair aglow, you knew it was more than the proverbial ships passing in the night. And the ships hadn't passed last night, either, had they?

She tried hard to focus on mundane, practical things. "I'm going to have to find another solution to my Christmas decoration problem. One that doesn't involve massacring something as majestic as your tree." She opened Maisie's door and bent down to give Muffin a scratch behind the ears. "Let's hope something comes to me. At the moment, I'm fresh out of ideas."

"You could go for lots of standard-sized Christmas trees in the hall and in the main rooms. I can easily supply those."

Lucy shook her head. "Wouldn't do. Our guests expect a bit of an extravaganza—the wow factor, you know?—and the trouble is that, when you've done it once, you have to keep doing it. And it has to be bigger, better, *wowier* every time. We had silver trees everywhere last year, don't you remember? Embossed on the soap. Sprayed on the windows. Even on the roof. How do I top that?"

"Gold trees?"

"Yeah, and diamond-encrusted ones next year? No. It mustn't be anything as predictable as that. Some of the guests have been regulars for three or four years. They expect to be surprised."

"I can think of one way to surprise them."

"Really? What?"

"Don't put up any decorations at all. No trees, no tinsel, nothing. That'd certainly surprise them."

"Too right." Lucy chuckled. "You really do hate Christmas, don't you, Gabe?" Then she sighed. "And if I don't come up with an idea soon, I'm probably going to hate it, too. Argh."

She gave Muffin a final pat, climbed into the driver's seat and put the key in the ignition.

"Actually, I might have an idea."

She turned back to him eagerly. "Tell me."

He leaned forward and stroked his fingers down her thigh. His touch shivered all the way down to her toes. They curled.

"Don't do that," she croaked. "Someone will see."

"No one can see. Only Muffin. And he won't tell." It was true. The door was only half open and his body filled the gap. Even dear-but-gossipy Jane wouldn't be able to see where his hand was. To prove his point, he did it again.

Lucy closed her eyes and swallowed hard. Resolving not to provoke him into further liberties—however much she was enjoying them—she said, "If you've really got an idea, tell me what it is. Please, Gabe."

He pulled back and grinned down at her. "Not sure it'll work yet. And I need to sort out a few things before I show you. Tell you what—why don't I came over to the Manor later and give you a demo? If Sir Drew will let me cross the threshold, that is."

"He will. We've, er, reached an understanding. And he's decided he doesn't want to break your lease. From what he said, he knows he was in the wrong, though he'll never admit it to you. But he's seeing his lawyer about it this afternoon. And he asked me to tell you the lease is safe."

185

"That's fantastic news. Thank you, Lucy. I'm sure I've got you to thank."

"I think Dad's conscience had more to do with it. Anyway, there won't be any awkwardness today. He's gone to meet a new client this morning. So he won't be around all day. Tell you what—why don't you come to lunch? We could have a picnic in the kitchen. And you could bring your mysterious solution with you."

Gabe checked his watch. "OK. It'll take me an hour or so to work things out. So not too early."

"One o'clock?"

He grinned. "Fine. I'll be there. With luck, I'll have the answer to a maiden's prayers piled in the back. Come on, Muffin. You can give me a hand."

Lucy mouth was so dry she couldn't speak. She nodded, started the engine and drove carefully back to the lane. The answer to a maiden's prayers? After those kisses in the arboretum, she knew precisely what that was. The man in the driver's seat.

# Chapter Seventeen

"ROASTED RED PEPPER AND tomato soup. With warm rosemary and walnut bread. And there's cheese and fruit to follow. Hope that's OK?" Lucy put a steaming pottery bowl on the kitchen table in front of Gabe. And then another for herself.

"It smells fantastic. Home-made, is it?"

"Yes."

When Gabe looked up enquiringly at her, Lucy shook her head. "Not by me, I'm afraid. When the chef is here, cooking for guests, he usually finds time to put some stuff in the freezer for me. The soup is his. So's the bread, actually."

Gabe took a spoonful of the soup, savouring its rich and subtle flavours. "Well, I don't care who made it, it's terrific. Especially on a cold winter's day. Warms the cockles, as they used to say."

They ate for a while in silence but, this time, it was not at all awkward.

Funny how they'd become so comfortable together in such a short time, Gabe thought. It was amazing what a little kissing could do for a relationship.

He smiled inwardly at the recollection, hoping it could be repeated soon.

"Gabe, I know you hate Christmas—I'm not that fond of it myself, to be honest—but I—"

"Why not? I thought all women loved Christmas. All those festive trappings and family feasts."

"Not for us. I… It's true that Dad and I like to have the house full for the festive season. But you may have noticed that it's always a business transaction. We reckon, well, if we're busy with the guests we can't think about all the traditional Christmas jollification. To be honest, there are some things about Christmas that I don't want to remember, ever again."

"Oh." He was shocked. "Want to talk about it?"

Lucy shook her head. "Not really. My mother died on Christmas Eve," she said baldly. "I'd rather not discuss that, if you don't mind. For us, Christmas is pretty bleak. You've never told me why you hate Christmas, either. Want to talk about it?"

She'd got him there. He might as well come clean. "It's straightforward enough. Christmas is a family thing. Children come home to their parents; or grandparents visit their grandchildren with heaps of presents and play Santa Claus and— Anyway, you can't do it if you don't have any family. And I don't have any family. I went to Jane's last year. It was incredibly kind of her and all her family. They did everything they could to make me welcome but—to be absolutely honest—it was grim. I hated every minute of it. I felt like a spare part. And I was."

"Yup. Know what you mean. Done that. Got several t-shirts."

"But you've got your father."

Surely that made all the difference?

"Yes. And he's got me. But that's it. So, as I said, we fill the house with wealthy guests and they enjoy themselves while we run ourselves ragged, making sure nothing goes wrong. It's a great way to pass the time. And before we know it, it's New Year and it's all over."

"Yes. I can see it would work." Maybe she would tell him more about her mother's death. Eventually. When she trusted him more. It sounded as though she could do with a listening ear. And possibly a shoulder to cry on, too.

"If you like, Gabe, you could come here for Christmas."

That was a surprise. Automatically, Gabe responded, "I don't think I—"

"It's not a family thing, as I said. If you came, you'd be one of the runners-around, like Dad and me. And it passes the time. Oh, and the food's great, because the chef does it all. Costs me an arm and two legs to get him to work over Christmas, but it's amazing what you can get if you pay enough." She grimaced.

"It's tempting. But it's not— Can I think about it, Lucy?"

"Sure." She waved her spoon in the air. "Just let me know if you want to join the mad Manor circus. No free-loading, mind. You'd have to earn your crust."

He chuckled. "I think I'm used to that, Lucy Cairns." He opened his hand, palm up, to show off his calluses.

"Yes, well, OK. Point taken." She grinned and went back to her soup.

"Right. Demo time. This is going to be a two-man, er, two-person job, Lucy. I do need your help here."

"Yes, but I don't understand—"

189

"Let's see if I can surprise you, shall we? You wanted your one Christmas tree to fill the middle of the main staircase, didn't you? Well, let's see if we can do something a bit different."

He led the way to the grand curving staircase and stood there, gazing assessingly at it. "Right. I'd like you to sit on the fifth stair up, please. And put your feet on the second stair. Can you reach? Oh well, the third will do for the demo."

Lucy did as she was told. When she frowned up at him, he grinned and wagged a finger at her. He was enjoying this. She felt like punching him, but she knew he'd only laugh, so she decided to bide her time.

He fetched two longish planks of wood that he'd propped up by the front door. "What I want you to do, Lucy, is put half of this under your bottom and poke the other half through the banister rails. And do the same with the second one, under your feet."

"But why?"

"As I told you before, Lucy—" he dropped a light kiss on her lips "—sometimes you talk too much. Wait and see."

"I'm certainly not going to be sitting on the stairs while the guests are running around the house. And not on top of a plank of wood, either."

He grinned. "No, I'm not suggesting that you do. This is just a mock-up, cobbled together to show you how it might work. I wasn't planning on planks across the stairs, I promise you. Now, wait there, and I'll show you how it works." He disappeared. A couple of minutes later, he was back, carrying two little potted Christmas trees, each no more than a couple of feet high.

"Right, Lucy. Now don't move. And make sure you put plenty of weight on your feet, or we're going to have a helluva mess on the floor." With that, he balanced one of the Christmas trees on the plank jutting out from under her bottom and the second on the plank held by her feet. "What do you think?"

"Um, it's a bit difficult to tell, from where I'm sitting."

He grinned. "Now, this is the bit I'm going to enjoy. If I just snuggle up next to you…"

He sat on the fifth stair and used his backside to push her across the plank until she was squashed right up against the banister.

"Hang on a minute. I can't breathe if you do that."

"I need to get two cheeks on so that it doesn't topple. Right. I'm there. And I've got the other one with my feet. You can get up now."

Lucy hardly had space to move. She managed to pull herself up using the banister for support.

Gabe, still grinning, wriggled even further towards the banister so that he was sitting where Lucy had been. His booted feet were firmly clamping the bottom plank to the stair.

"Now, go and stand in the hall, and see what you think."

She did. "Well…"

"You have to use a bit of imagination here. It won't be planks, of course. We'd have little stands attached to the side of the stairs. And the trees would go all the way up the inside curve of the staircase, one every three or four steps. Not too close together. We'd want them to be seen as individual trees, but also as a pattern. And you'd want lights on them. I'm sure we could string little LEDs round them all. In the dark, it would look pretty good, I think. Tiny starlit trees spiralling all the way up to the fourth floor. What d'you think?"

She thought it would be magical.

191

But she wasn't ready to tell him so. Not yet. She stuck to the prosaic. "We'd have to water them. How would we do that?"

He laughed. "What a practical woman you are, Lucy Cairns. Actually I have thought about that. If we fasten plastic-lined cachepots to the little wooden supports, we could be sure they wouldn't leak and we'd be able to put the pots with the trees inside them. The cachepots can be as fancy as you like. All we'd have to do would be to go around with a watering can in the mornings, before the guests were up and about. Simple, eh?"

Actually, it was brilliant. And the effect would be, could be, like something out of a fairytale.

"Mmm. If I got the cachepots painted silver, I could put white lights on the trees and it would all reflect beautifully. It would be like thousands of stars, sweeping up to the heavens." She clapped her hands. "It's a fantastic idea, Gabe."

He bowed. Unfortunately, that took some of the weight off the upper plank and the tree wobbled dangerously. Both of them tried to grab it before it fell. Gabe succeeded. And managed to catch Lucy's hands in the process. He stroked her fingers, murmuring appreciatively.

Lucy tried to ignore his touch. "I think this one would be safer on the floor." She lifted the little pot and put it down by the front door. Then she did the same with the one supported by Gabe's feet. "How many have you got, Gabe? The stairs go up for forty feet, remember, and there's an awful lot of banister."

"I had a couple of dozen ready for sale, though nobody's bought any yet. But I do actually have more. They're not as perfectly shaped, but if we put the best ones down here we could use the less symmetrical ones nearer the top. Your guests won't go all the way up there, will they?"

"Some of them will. Some of them will have rooms up there. But it doesn't matter. If we light it properly, they'll be mesmerised by the effect and they won't notice. Near the top, we can put the best side facing inwards towards the stairs, can't we?"

"Yeah, that should work. Now, about the stands. I need to—"

"You don't need to do anything except make me a drawing of what a stand should look like, and the dimensions. Then we can work out how many we need. I'll get Dad's carpenters to make them. They'll fit them too, if I ask nicely. Dad's electricians can sort the battery fixings for the LEDs. I don't want trailing wires everywhere."

"And I suppose you have someone who can produce forty silver cachepots at the drop of a hat?"

"Um, possibly. It's amazing what you can do with spray paint, you know."

He laughed. "Yes, OK. Well, find me some paper and I'll provide your drawing."

Lucy's work mobile rang while she was finishing the first coat on the cachepots. She had to strip off her paint-spattered rubber gloves before she could dig into her pocket for it. And then she had to pull off her mask in order to speak. Luckily, her caller hadn't rung off.

"Lucy Cairns."

"Lucy, it's Gabe. Where are you?"

She snorted. "I'm in the outhouse, spray-painting cachepots. I seem to have got more silver on me than on the pots."

"Excellent. I—"

"What do you mean, *excellent*? Are you happy that I'm covered in paint? And probably inhaling all sorts of noxious fumes in the process?" She was deliberately over-egging it. She was wearing old overalls. And she had the face mask to deal with the fumes. But she didn't have to tell Gabe all that.

"It's excellent because I'm ringing about your cachepots. I need to know how big they are."

Oh. "About ten inches across and twelve deep, at a guess. Do you need exact dimensions?"

"No. You've got a good eye."

"Why did you want to know, anyway?"

"Because I'm repotting all the little trees. The existing pots are too small and the trees would sit too far down in cachepots that big. The branches would be resting on the sides, too. Difficult for watering. And it would look amateurish. So I'm repotting the trees into bigger pots. They'll look better and they'll fit the cachepots. The extra compost will hold the water better, too."

"Yes, I see. Makes sense, I suppose."

"You bet your life it makes sense, ducky. I'm a nurseryman, remember? It's my job to know such things." He chuckled. "Same as it's your job to know about spray-painting. How far have you got, painted lady?"

She ignored the jibe. "I've done the first coat on all but two. Once they're all dry, I'll do second coats on all forty of them. Boring, but not difficult."

"I could say the same for repotting trees, except that it's not actually boring. I like getting my hands in moist compost like this. It's good stuff, I can promise you. Well, it should be, since I made it myself. You can pick it up in handfuls and trickle it between the tree roots." Lucy was sure he was doing precisely that as he spoke.

"And you know the roots appreciate it, too. The trees—
Oh." He broke off. Lucy could hear him scrabbling
about. "That's odd."

Odd? That sounded ominous to Lucy. "What? You
haven't broken one, have you, Gabe? We need every one
you've got."

"The trees will all be fine, I promise. Worry not. I'll
bring them over later, once I've given them a good
watering. How're the carpenters getting on?"

"Nearly done. We'll soon have forty elegant little
platforms, waiting to receive their trees. And the
electrics are nearly done, too. These new battery-
operated LEDs are great. You can run the lights for
ninety hours non-stop so we won't have to be changing
batteries while the guests are here. Good, eh?"

"I get the message. So the only chore will be watering
the trees."

"And running around after all our guests." Lucy
growled a little. "I shouldn't complain. I was the one who
organised it all. So I'll just have to suck it up, won't I?"

"Just don't suck up any silver paint, OK? See you
later." He rang off so quickly that Lucy couldn't reply.

They hadn't been an item for very long, but Lucy
knew Gabe of old. He was hiding something, or plotting
something, or both. She hoped it wouldn't muck up her
plans. As long as she got her forty trees, she could cope
with anything else he threw at her.

Couldn't she?

Gabe found Lucy in the kitchen. She was wearing the
most disreputable overalls he had ever seen. And she had
spots of silver paint on her face. She looked good
enough to eat.

"Hello, gorgeous." He picked her up and swung her

195

round. "Your trees are here."

"All of them?" she asked suspiciously.

"Course. Took me two trips but all forty are outside. You can inspect them if you don't believe me. And, by the way, you've got paint on your forehead."

"I think I've got paint everywhere. In spite of a headscarf and a face mask. I'll have to try to scrub it all off in the shower tonight."

That sounded interesting. "Need any help with that?"

"Not tonight, thank you," she replied, primly.

"Pity." He took her hand and scrutinised it. It was grubby, but cleaner than the overalls. He supposed she'd been wearing gloves. "You've got pretty hands, Lucy. But they're quite workmanlike, too."

"You mean they're a bit square and my fingers are stubby. I know that. What's made you so interested in the shape of my hands all of a sudden?"

"Because—" he dug into his pocket "—I found this." He opened his fist. On it lay a tiny gold ring.

Lucy gasped.

"I ought to take it to the police," Gabe went on. "Someone must be missing it. But if it had fitted your hands, I might have been tempted to—"

Lucy found her voice at last. "It's my mum's wedding ring." She grabbed it and took it over to the window where the light was better. "Yes, look. There's an inscription inside. *M & A*, see? And the date of their wedding." She threw her arms round Gabe and hugged him. "Oh Gabe, I love you to bits. This is the best thing you could ever have done for me."

"I don't understand," he said slowly. "How on earth could your mother's wedding ring end up in my compost heap?"

"I don't know. And I don't care. But having it back—"

She danced around the room, holding the ring up in the air like a trophy.

He caught her and held her. "Well, I care. Explain please. Or do I have to riddle every bucketful of compost I've made in case there's more treasure in it?"

Lucy laughed. "No. There's no more. Not where this came from, anyway. The truth is: I lost it, years ago, somewhere on the estate. When I was just a kid. I can only assume that you gathered it up with your leaf mould. You do bag a lot of that, don't you? From all across the estate?"

Gabe nodded. "So what happens now then?"

"Now I give it back to Dad. And with luck he finally forgives me for having lost it. He told me last week he was planning to use the gold to make a new ring for himself, as a tribute to Mum. That was when he found out I'd lost it. That was when we had that blazing row. When he finally came back and yelled at you, it was me he really wanted to yell at. Oh Gabe, you're such a star." She made for the door. "I must go and tell Mum."

"But your mother isn't here. I mean, she's—"

"She's been dead a long time. Yes. But her portrait's hanging in my office and, when I'm on my own, I, um, I quite often talk to her."

Gabe shook his head in disbelief but he followed Lucy to her office. He found her standing by the fireplace, looking up at the portrait, and talking about the ring. "Does she talk back, at all?" he asked.

"No. But sometimes I think I see a sparkle in her eyes. And if you look closely, you'll see that the wedding ring on her finger is unusually bright today." She pointed.

"Aren't all rings painted bright yellow like that?"

Lucy shook her head. "No. In the picture, it was

197

fading away. But now it's back, in the portrait and in the flesh too. Oh Gabe, thank you. Thank you."

"You're welcome. What shall we do to celebrate? *The Feathers?*"

"Too public. And there are too many of Dad's people in the Manor, at the moment. If we're going to celebrate our, er, our reunion, I'd like it to be in private, wouldn't you?" She smiled mischievously up at him. "What time does Jane go home?"


It was the day before Christmas Eve and their tree display was finished. Gabe and Lucy, standing in the hall, craned their necks to see to the top of the staircase.

"It is magical." Lucy reached for Gabe's hand and squeezed it. "Like having my own private sky with my own glittering stars. It's astonishing."

"It's worked out much better than I thought it would. Something to do with the height, I suppose. Forty feet of twinkling lights is certainly impressive. I imagine your guests will be captivated."

Lucy turned to him and slid her hands round his neck. "And are you captivated, too, Gabe?"

"Not only with the lights." He wrapped his arms round her and pulled her closer. "D'you know, when I look into your eyes, I can see thousands of little white stars, sparkling there."

"That sounds very peculiar."

"No, it's enchanting." He kissed her. Thoroughly.

"Does that mean you *will* be staying here for Christmas?"

"I...well, someone has to water the trees, I suppose."

"I promise I'll make sure you do, you ratbag. I'll kick you out at crack of sparrows every morning to be on watering duties."

"Kick me out? Er, where from, exactly?"

"Ah. There's one thing I forgot to mention." She could feel herself reddening, in spite of the fact that they had already celebrated their Christmas reunion in a most satisfactory way. "We do have a lot of guests coming tomorrow and all the bedrooms are taken. You'll, um, you'll have to share mine for the duration. I hope you don't mind?"

He beamed at her. "I knew there was a reason for all those twinkling stars in your eyes. You're either a fairy, Lucy Cairns, or a witch. But, whichever you are, you've done the spell bit and I am totally enchanted. I don't mind in the least." He gave her a look that shivered all the way down to her toes. "In fact, I'm looking forward to it. Very much."

Lucy couldn't think of a word to say.

Gabe was gazing up at the spiral of trees again. "I wonder what you'll do next year, Lucy Cairns. This will take a bit of beating."

"I think that, next year, I'll be saying *Christmas is cancelled*." She looked up at her thousands of stars. A warm glow wrapped itself round her like soft cashmere. "I don't want to try to outdo this. It's magic. So maybe next year we can drop Christmas at the Manor and string a million lights round that eighty-footer in your arboretum instead. What do you think?"

"Yes, that's a great idea. There's just one problem."

He didn't say anything more. He was gazing down at her, his eyes dark.

Trying to stay practical, Lucy opened her mouth to ask what he was on about. Big mistake. Gabe took it as an invitation. He began to kiss her again. At the first touch of his lips, she forgot everything. She could feel herself floating up into her starry heaven.

Much later, they pulled apart. A little. It was blissful standing there with Gabe's arms round her. She was still floating, but memory prodded insistently at her. Ah yes. "You said there was a problem?"

"There is, but I've got the answer. Every grand Christmas tree needs a fairy on the top. Even eighty-footers. So I hope you've got a head for heights."

Lucy did punch him then. It made no impression, of course. He caught her up in his arms and whirled her round and round until she was too dizzy to speak. When he eventually put her down, she had to grab the banister to keep her balance. "I'll give you fairies, Gabriel Bliss," she managed at last, trying to look stern and raising the clenched fist she knew she wouldn't use again.

"I hope you will, love." His dark gaze caressed her face for long seconds. Then he put an arm round her waist. "If I'm to share your room tonight, hadn't you better show me where it is?"

"I have my own flat in the east wing. It's, er, totally private. No one comes in unless I invite them."

"Not even your father?"

"Especially not my father." She made a face. Then she grinned at him. "It's even more private than your place at the nursery. No one will interrupt us. So would you like to come up and, er, recce where you'll be staying? I don't have anything else to do for the next hour or two."

"Funnily enough," he said, with something of a catch in his voice, "neither have I."

## THE END

### *Dear Reader : From Joanna Maitland*

This was my second venture into timeslip—you can read an extract from the first, *Lady in Lace*, at the end of this book—and so, if you enjoyed this story, I'd be really grateful if you could leave a review at your usual online store or on your favourite reader website. Your review can help other readers to find and enjoy my books, too.

Thank you!

### *For Competitions, Giveaways and Other Stuff*

For news, free stories, competitions and giveaways, and lots of fun stuff, please visit the multi-author website at Libertà Books https://libertabooks.com where you can have your say on the weekly blog, or maybe write a love letter to a favourite novel. Intrigued? Have a look and see whether you would like to join in. You'd be most welcome. We often host writers you will know and we talk about all sorts of books which probably include many of your favourites.

Do come and join the fun in the Libertà hive where readers and authors chat and laugh about books, films, history, costume, the craft of writing and much, much more.

The Libertà hive tweets @LibertaBooks and you can find us on FaceBook/libertabooks, too.

My old joannamaitland.com website is no longer available. Information about me and my books is now all on my Libertà page at libertabooks.com/joanna. Or you can follow me on Twitter @JoannaMaitland to get all my latest news.

# About the Author

Joanna Maitland has published 13 Regency historicals with Harlequin Mills & Boon since 2000 and has sold about one and a half million copies around the world, with readers in countries as diverse as Japan and Brazil. She is now an independently published author. She is continuing to write Regencies, but also hopping over the hedge into lush new pastures. She has published two timeslip romances so far: *Lady in Lace* and *To a Blissful Christmas Reunion.* She has also published her first vampire comedy romance: *I, Vampire* in the Libertà Books anthology *Beach Hut Surprise*. There will more timeslips and romances in the future. There will probably be more vampires, too, because Joanna has fallen in love with Theo, her vampire hero.

Joanna is one of the founding partners of Libertà Books, a multi-author website at https://libertabooks.com/ where readers and authors share their love of books, reading, and fun. She is also a proud and long-standing member of the Romantic Novelists' Association which has honoured her by making her a Vice President of the Association.

# *Lady in Lace*

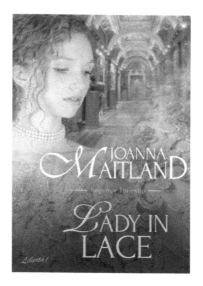

## A shredded gold lace ballgown.
## The greatest rake in Regency London.
## And the modern woman who links them both.

When costume curator Emma Stanley meets a frock-coated phantom in
an endless museum passage, her body takes fire at his touch. But he
melts away, leaving her lost, and clutching the shredded gold lace of a
Regency ballgown.

The magic of the ballgown transports Emma across centuries. When is
she? Where is she? Most importantly, *who* is she in this alien time?

In front of her, a naked man rises from his bath. He welcomes her. He
knows her name. He wants her. But he's dangerous—the greatest rake in
Regency London, the stud that every woman desires.

Should Emma respond to him? Will she get back to her own time if she
does? And, given the threatening shadows swirling round in her modern
world, is it safe to return?

*Read on for an extract*

# LADY IN LACE
## Chapter One

EMMA WAS ALONE IN the passage. She hadn't been down here since her first day. She remembered being shown round then, peering into all these museum store rooms. Today it felt different. Was it because it was so late? But surely it hadn't been this gloomy down here before? Or this cold?

A strange shiver danced down her spine. That mahogany door. She hadn't noticed it before. It seemed totally out of place in a museum. But it was real. Solid.

She paused in the act of reaching for the intricate brass handle. She could just about make out her own frozen shape, dimly reflected in the door's fielded panels. There was something ghostly about her fuzzy outline, as if it were half real, half melting.

Nonsense. It was just a door. If she wanted to know where it led, she would have to open it.

Her extended arm seemed reluctant to make that last effort, her fingers unwilling to grasp the cold metal. That strange shiver came again, this time tingling down her arm and into her outstretched fingers. For a single mad moment, she thought she saw... She could have sworn she saw jagged streaks of blue lightning joining her hand to the brass.

*Too much wine last night*, she told herself sternly, trying to dismiss the weird feelings. *Or those mussels. You should never trust mussels.*

She forced her rigid body to move. Only a wimp would be frightened off by a dim reflection and a slightly queasy stomach. And she'd promised herself she wouldn't be a coward any more. Hadn't she?

She grasped the handle at last. It was strangely cold, almost icy. She shuddered again, but refused to let go. She began to turn it, to pull the door open.

Immediately, too soon, the door began to swing towards her, as if it had a mind of its own. Under her fingers, the metal began to heat.

Emma gasped in shock and snatched her hand away. In less than a second, the brass had become too hot to touch. It was impossible. Cold... hot... blue lightning? Was she in the middle of some strange dream? Would she wake up soon?

The door had swung open on silent hinges. Expectantly. Waiting for her to step inside. Into the louring darkness beyond.

*I am not afraid of you, whatever you are.* She had taught herself to conquer her fears. She would not stand here on the threshold, petrified, like some kind of statue.

"Damn those mussels," she spat. Her wild words seemed to echo for a second. Then they were swallowed up by the dark silence in front of her. But they had broken the spell. She could move at last. And it would be forward. She was her own woman now. She would not run ever again.

She took two firm steps through the doorway. Into the gloom.

Why was it so dark? A room, even a corridor, should have windows somewhere. Even here in the museum. What was this place?

She stood still, trying to make sense of her surroundings. Behind her was the open door and the dim light of the hallway. In front, nothing. Or so it seemed. Yet she sensed that there was a great space in front of her, as if this darkness went on and on.

For the moment, her eyes were worse than useless. She reached her arms out sideways, feeling for walls. If this were merely a dark corridor, there should be walls.

Her right hand met something soft. Yielding. At her touch, it swung away.

She cried out, "Who's there?"

The softness swung back against her hand. Pile. Velvet? But not alive at all. She understood that instinctively, even in the dark, for there was no smell of life. It was some kind of velvet wrap, suspended here, swaying at her touch.

Not a corridor, then. A storage cupboard? But why so enormous?

She was beginning to overcome her childish fancies at last. Her mysterious door led to a huge cupboard, big enough to walk into. She put both hands on the velvet and groped her way towards a hanger and a rail, then on to more hangers and more suspended garments: furs, heavy wool, then fine silk and gauze. It was an enormous clothes store.

But whose clothes? This was no way to store museum exhibits.

She was finally beginning to see through the gloom,

helped by the faint light from the hall at her back. The racks of hanging garments stretched into the distance and disappeared. As if the rail went on for ever.

She forced herself to straighten her shoulders. She would not be intimidated by a mere cupboard. She lifted her chin and took a deep breath, ready to challenge anything. Anyone.

She could smell the sea.

Impossible. Her mind was playing tricks. It had to be that. Didn't it?

She could smell the sea. As strongly as if she were standing on a beach, with banks of drying kelp and crashing breakers.

Her shoes began to sink into soft sand. Her toes curled automatically, trying for grip. She grabbed for the coat rail, desperate to keep her balance.

The coat rail was gone.

Her flailing arms met wool, warm wool, and warm flesh beneath.

"Take care, or you will fall." It was a man's voice, strong and reassuring. It seemed familiar. As did his touch.

Her body knew him. This time, she was not afraid.

She had come home at last.

She had been holding her breath, desperately trying to fathom what was happening to her. Now, relaxing, she breathed in the comforting scents of sand and sea and warm, living man. He smelt of fresh winds and freedom. His touch, where he held her up, was merely a polite support. Yet it was more, too. A caress, a knowing caress, of two bodies that had lain together, naked skin against naked skin.

So familiar. So loved. And yet she did not know him.

She tried to speak, but her throat would not open. She

reached for him with her free hand, clutching for his arm where he held her up, and beyond, to the body she longed to find. It was eluding her.

"Oh, where are you, my love?" she managed at last, in a voice that sounded nothing like her own. Had she really said those words? To a man she didn't know?

His reply was wordless, a soft laugh deep in his chest. Then the contact was broken. The warmth of him was gone.

She was alone.

The ground beneath her feet was solid again.

He was gone. And so was the smell of the sea.

Tears of frustration welled up in her straining eyes. Her lover, her life, the man she was destined for—he had been here, holding her. Then, so swiftly, he was gone.

She peered into the darkness, narrowing her eyes. Surely there was movement, somewhere in the distance? A shadow, a shape. Yes, someone was there. He was still with her.

"Don't go, my love. Please don't leave me." She spoke without hesitation this time. Her heart was pounding like a racing engine. It was vital not to lose him. He had to understand that she was his. Always.

That deep laugh again, but no words. She saw the dim shape of a tall man in some kind of tail coat. For a split second, she caught the gleam of something gold before he turned away. And a flash of white teeth as he smiled back at her.

No need for words. His smile said it all. *Wait for me, love. We will meet again.*

She started towards him, arms outstretched to embrace his beloved form. Her questing hands met another rack of clothes, soft, and full, and yielding. But lifeless.

He had been here, touching her, reaching for her. She could have been safe in his arms. Should have been. But now he was gone. And her heart was empty.

She clung to the rail, racked by sudden shuddering sobs. Nothing she had suffered could begin to approach this searing emotion, this harrowing sense of loss. As if her heart had been torn from her living body and trampled in the dirt.

Under her hand, something scratched her skin.

Beckoning.

It was ridiculous to think that racks of clothes could call to her, but she was prepared to believe almost anything now. She stroked a hand blindly across the hanger. This was a flimsy gown made of something she could not identify. Fairy gauze? Nothing could surprise her any more.

She made to lift the hanger from the rail. It stuck. She leaned closer, determined not to be beaten. It had summoned her, so she would have it.

It smelled of the sea.

For a second only, and the scent was gone. Then the gown came sweetly into her hands, as if it had leapt from the rail of its own volition. As if it were alive.

She brought it to her face, to touch, to caress, to breathe in its elusive scent. Her love came with the sea, and this gown was the link.

The gown's own scent was almost too faint to discern.

It was not the sea after all. It was lavender.


"What have you got there, Emma?"

She was standing in the passageway, gazing down at the golden lace and gauze draped over her arms. But she had been somewhere else entirely.

"Emma?" It was Richard, another of the museum

curators, one who had begun to feel like a friend in spite of the difference in their ages. "Are you OK?"

She looked at the golden gown, then at Richard, and then swung round to the wall behind her. Yes, there was a door. No, it wasn't made of mahogany. It was a standard museum door, one she had definitely seen before. It led to the racks where they stored the costume collection in specially controlled conditions. "I...I...I'm fine. It was just this gown. It—"

His frown evaporated. "Oh, yes. That one. Your predecessor showed it to me once. Shame it's in such a state. It must have been stunning when it was new. What date do you reckon it is?"

Emma stared at him and then glanced down at the dress. "Er, middle to late Regency, I think. Somewhere between 1815 and 1820." She looked again, really looking this time. Just minutes ago, in the gloom, it had been floating on that hanger like woven gossamer in a summer breeze. But the gown in her arms was little more than shreds of golden overskirts, suspended from a fragile lace bodice and a silken petticoat. One puff sleeve was almost intact; the other was a wreck.

"I'd have thought it was beyond restoration," Richard said with a knowledgeable nod, "but you're the expert. It would be great if you could put it on display. Regency exhibits always pull in the punters. It's all those Jane Austen fans, I suppose."

"And memories of Colin Firth in a wet shirt," Emma quipped with a smile, glad to be brought back to earth again.

Richard raised his eyebrows. Well, he was a man and well past forty. He probably wouldn't understand how that iconic TV adaptation could feed fantasies, more than twenty years on.

A fantasy? Was that what she'd had? It had seemed so real. You didn't smell lavender in fantasies, did you? Or the sea? Or—?

She banished the image of white teeth and glinting gold to the back of her mind. She was a serious woman, with an important new job here. And a whole new life.

"I'm going to have a look at it under the lights in the research room," she announced in her best reliable-colleague voice. "Need the magnifiers to see exactly how bad the damage is. We might be able to do something. You never know." She turned and started along the corridor. Then she remembered how late it was. "There's time before we have to lock up, isn't there?" she called over her shoulder. Richard, as the longest-serving curator, was responsible for locking up the museum at the end of the day. He replied with a cheery wave.

She was still examining the gown when closing time actually came. She wanted to weep over it. Under the magnifiers, she had discovered, with a shock, that at least some of the rents were not caused by age or vermin. Some of the gold lace had been cut. Someone—someone out of their mind, surely?—had taken a knife or scissors to this fairytale ballgown and deliberately shredded the overskirt. Someone had wanted to be sure this gown could never be worn again.

Someone hateful.

She leaned back in her chair and began to muse on the owner of the gown. The museum had no information about who she might have been. It would have been someone rich, perhaps aristocratic. Young, but not too young. Really young girls wore white ballgowns in those days. This one probably belonged to a married lady. A rich, young, married lady. Was it her husband who had destroyed the gown? Had he found her in some compromising—?

"Emma?" It was Richard, doing his final rounds to check everything was locked away. "Oh. I didn't realise you still had that gown out." He muttered a curse. "I've locked all the stores." He glanced across at the clock on the church opposite the museum. He was due to meet his wife and baby daughter immediately after work, Emma knew. He wouldn't want to keep them waiting in the cold. It was spring, but the wind was bitter.

Emma leapt to her feet, conscience-stricken. It would take a good ten minutes to open up the stores again. "I'm sorry, Richard. I lost track. Look, it's about time I took a turn at locking up, anyway. Has everyone else gone?" When he nodded, she said decisively, "Fine, well, leave me the keys and I'll finish doing the security checks after I've put this away. I know how to set the alarms. You can rely on me."

He chuckled. "You do realise you'll have to be first in tomorrow if you have the keys? I thought you weren't a morning person?"

She smiled at him. "It's amazing what caffeine can do, you know."

He looked relieved as he tossed her the huge bunch of keys. "See you tomorrow then. Early. *Very* early." He was still smiling as he left.

Emma laid the keys on the big round table and sat down again to gaze at the gown. Silence settled. Richard had switched off most of the lights. It was like being on an island of light surrounded by darkness.

She could smell the sea.

Rubbish. She was nowhere near the sea. It must be simply that idiotic idea of being on an island. Islands were surrounded by sea, not darkness. So she had *fancied* she smelt it. Was she going down with something, maybe?

She touched the back of her hand to her forehead. It felt normal. Well, it would, wouldn't it? You could never feel your own fever.

*Get back to work, Emma Stanley,* she told herself. *You are supposed to be a sensible, dependable, professional woman. Put the gown away, lock up the building, and go home. You can always check your temperature once you're there.*

It didn't matter if she had a temperature like a furnace tomorrow morning. She was in charge of the keys now. No matter what, she would have to be here early enough to open up.


The clock of St Mary's struck the half hour.

Shocked back to reality, Emma gasped aloud. How long had she been sitting here in the research room, marvelling at the shredded beauty of the golden gown?

She shook her head in disbelief at her own strange behaviour. She had won the job of regional costume curator because of her innovative but level-headed approach to planning the future of the collection. Her ideas and passion had persuaded the panel to overlook her patchy employment record.

Yet here she was, barely a few weeks into her new job, and without a single level-headed thought in her mind.

She was seeing things, and feeling things, and, most outrageous of all, smelling things that could not possibly be real.

She lurched to her feet, toppling her chair in her haste. She had to put the gown away safely in the storeroom. But first, she would put a little distance between them. To catch her breath. She would go and change into her travelling clothes. A splash of cold water on her face and neck might help, too. Anything to bring her back to reality.

A few minutes later, Emma was smoothing her navy pencil skirt onto its hanger. That suit had been a good buy, in spite of the high cost. Creases fell out of the material when it was hung up and the cut flattered her figure, even though the suit was now a little loose. She had lost a lot of weight during the long months of her hellish divorce, but she had resolved to fix that. From now on, she would eat regularly, and properly. She had a new career and a bold new life, and she was going to make a success of both. There was no one trying to control her any more and she would never, *never* let it happen again.

She took a step back and gazed at her reflection in the long mirror. Much too thin, but otherwise not bad. Her dark red hair, definitely her best feature, was piled on top of her head in loose curls, in vague imitation of the Regency styles she had always admired. Her new gold underwear looked classy and flattering.

A strange coincidence that she had chosen to wear gold today, the same colour as that amazing Regency gown. Almost as if she had been meant to try it on…

Barely a minute later, Emma found herself back in the research room with the damaged gown in her hands. It would do no harm to try it on, just for a moment or two, just to see how it looked. And then she would return it reverently to the store room and never be tempted again.

The bell of St Mary's began to toll. It was almost seven. Where on earth had the time gone?

All the same, it was not too late just to…

With infinite care, Emma started to push an arm into

the undamaged sleeve.

Blue lightning shot along her arm. It should have burned, but instead it was freezing cold. A moment later, Emma felt a whoosh of icy air howling through the room, like the bitterest Arctic gale. The noise was even worse than the cold. It sounded as if some hideous giant was sucking the life out of everything, swallowing it down into consuming darkness. Emma cried out in terror. At least, she tried to. But her voice was sucked into the void along with everything else.

She was in the dark. She was falling.

And she was alone.

*LADY IN LACE*
is available as an ebook from your local Amazon
Also available in paperback from all good bookshops
ISBN 978-0-9957046-5-7

# Stories by Joanna Maitland

**Unsuitable Matches Series**
A Penniless Prospect
Marrying the Major*
Rake's Reward*

**Star Crossed Lovers Series**
My Lady Angel*
The Solway Bride*
Star Crossed at Twilight*

**The Aikenhead Honours Series**
His Cavalry Lady*
His Reluctant Mistress*
His Forbidden Liaison*
His Silken Seduction*

**Individual Titles**
A Poor Relation
The Mystery Mistletoe Bride*
A Regency Invitation
[with Nicola Cornick & Elizabeth Rolls]

**Timeslip Romances**
Lady in Lace*
To a Blissful Christmas Reunion*

**Romantic Comedy**
I, Vampire*
[in Libertà Books' *Beach Hut Surprise* Anthology]

*published by Joanna Maitland Independent

Lightning Source UK Ltd.
Milton Keynes UK
UKHW010229101022
410220UK00005B/75